TODAY'S SPECIAL

The man turned as the woman grabbed his arm at the elbow and prevented him from drawing his pistol.

"Is there some misunderstanding here, Luke?" she said, staring directly into Slocum's eyes. The man she had called Luke wrenched his arm from her grasp and his hand dove like a hawk toward his pistol.

At the same time, he stepped behind the woman, putting her between him and his target, Slocum.

In that split second, Slocum made his decision. Two people might die real sudden, but he was not going to be one of them. His eyes narrowed to hard, dark slits and he went into a fighting crouch as his hand streaked like lightning toward the Colt .45 on his gunbelt.

All of the air seemed to have been sucked out of the room as the patrons froze like statues, waiting for the death roar of gunfire . . .

AND THE TETON TEMPTRESS

J

JOVE BOOKS, NEW YORK

THE BERKLEY PUBLISHING GROUP
Published by the Penguin Group
Penguin Group (USA) Inc.
375 Hudson Street, New York, New York 10014, USA
Penguin Group (Canada), 10 Alcorn Avenue, Toronto, Ontario M4V 3B2, Canada
(a division of Pearson Penguin Canada Inc.)
Penguin Books Ltd., 80 Strand, London WC2R 0RL, England
Penguin Group Ireland, 25 St. Stephen's Green, Dublin 2, Ireland (a division of Penguin Books Ltd.)
Penguin Group (Australia), 250 Camberwell Road, Camberwell, Victoria 3124, Australia
(a division of Pearson Australia Group Pty. Ltd.)
Penguin Books India Pvt. Ltd., 11 Community Centre, Panchsheel Park, New Delhi—110 017, India
Penguin Group (NZ), Cnr. Airborne and Rosedale Roads, Albany, Auckland 1310, New Zealand
(a division of Pearson New Zealand Ltd.)
Penguin Books (South Africa) (Pty.) Ltd., 24 Sturdee Avenue, Rosebank, Johannesburg 2196, South Africa

Penguin Books Ltd., Registered Offices: 80 Strand, London WC2R 0RL, England

SLOCUM AND THE TETON TEMPTRESS

A Jove Book / published by arrangement with the author

PRINTING HISTORY
Jove edition / December 2004

For information address: The Berkley Publishing Group,
a division of Penguin Group (USA) Inc.,
375 Hudson Street, New York, New York 10014.

ISBN: 0-515-13858-4

JOVE®
Jove Books are published by The Berkley Publishing Group,
a division of Penguin Group (USA) Inc.
375 Hudson Street, New York, New York 10014.
JOVE is a registered trademark of Penguin Group (USA) Inc.
The "J" design is a trademark belonging to Penguin Group (USA) Inc.

PRINTED IN THE UNITED STATES OF AMERICA

10 9 8 7 6 5 4 3 2 1

1

Slocum cursed the cutting wind that sprang up as soon as he had stopped to make camp. Even though he wore a heavy coat he had bought when he outfitted in Cheyenne, the wind's icy fingers slipped through the horn buttonholes and the front flap. He pulled up the fur collar so that his neck was protected from the scathing blasts of frosty air that flew down from the high peaks of the majestic Grand Tetons.

He found a place off the trail, nestled in between huge boulders that formed a shelter. He hobbled all four horses, the one he was riding, Oro, a tall golden sorrel gelding, and the three he was taking up to the Hole, two of them serving as packhorses. They were of good Arabian/Morgan stock, handpicked in Denver and now trail-seasoned, but skittery in the wind that howled and whistled and roared out of the north.

He scooped out a hollow in the soft earth to form a fire ring. It was not yet winter, but summer in the high country was now only a memory. He placed small stones around the depression to block the wind and began gathering firewood, starting with small twigs of dead juniper and manzanita, then adding larger chunks to lay on after he got the fire started. The nearby juniper tree had been smashed by the horns of a bull elk in the rut long ago. The tree looked as if it had been blasted by a grenade or a cannonball, its twisted limbs torn asunder by the ravishing tines of huge antlers.

His hands were cold when he finished gathering wood and he squatted next to the fire and warmed them over the licking flames. He gathered more stones and stacked them on one side of the fire so that it would reflect the heat to that place where he laid out his bedroll, next to one of the large boulders. He unsaddled his horse and brought the saddle, bags and the '73 Winchester in its sheath back to his camp, and arranged them so that the saddle acted as another buffer against the wind, and the rifle, in its scabbard, was within easy reach. He rummaged through his saddlebags and laid out a small pot with a handle, a small skillet, a tin of grease, flour, coffee, dried beef, a couple of small onions and a potato that was about to spoil on him.

He figured he was no more than a half day or a day out of Jackson, but if he continued his climb, he would be riding straight into the teeth of the wind and lose more time than he would gain. He had some daylight time left, and he wouldn't start supper until he was satisfied with the size of the fire. He fed wood to it and watched it burn down. But he never looked too long at the flames. In wild country, a man had to keep his wits about him and be able to see. He looked away from the fire and back up at the towering Tetons, their snowcapped peaks obscured by white clouds.

As Slocum squatted by the blazing fire, he dug inside his coat to his shirt pocket and took out the letter he had received from his friend, Hovis Benton. The paper was showing signs of wear, because he had pored over it many times over the past several weeks, trying to decipher the meaning between the lines.

He read Hovis' words again, shielding the missive from the wind.

> *"Dear Johnny: Come quick to Jackson Hole in the Grand Tetons. I think I'm in big trouble. Something I found out. Bring extra horses if you can. I'm staying at Mrs. Fletcher's Boarding House. If not there, I work at the Silvertip Saloon. I hope you can come real soon or I might wind up plumb dead. Thanks, friend. Hovis."*

It was a puzzling note to Slocum because Hovis did not tell him how many horses to bring or what kind of trouble he was in. And Jackson Hole was a mighty tough place to get to, especially with winter breathing down his neck. But Hovis was a good man and not taken to flights of fancy. If he said he was in trouble, then he was. If he felt he was in danger of being killed, then Slocum had to take him seriously.

Three horses were as many as Slocum thought he could handle in that rough country, riding alone. He figured if Hovis wanted to go somewhere into the wilderness, they could each ride one horse and use the two extra horses for pack animals and spare mounts.

"Damn it, Hove," Slocum said aloud, as he put the letter back in his pocket, "what in hell is going on?"

His words to himself were snatched away by a gust of wind, as lost on his ears as they were on Benton's.

Slocum heard one of the horses whicker and he looked up. The horses stood like statues, facing the mountain range, their ears hardened to cones, twisting to pick up any sound. Slocum stood up and stared off in the same direction. The road wound out of a curve and was empty. But something was up there, he knew. It could be a grizzly, a mountain lion, an elk, a mule deer. Something.

The horses' legs quivered as they stood like silent equine statues, every muscle quivering under their hides as if they had been galvanized by an electric shock.

Slocum stood up and moved away from the fire toward the boulder where his rifle lay in its scabbard. He hunkered down and slipped the Winchester from its sheath. He stood up again and moved behind another boulder, levering a cartridge into the firing chamber with slow precision. The rifle cocked as the round seated and he pulled the lever back up tight against the stock. He slid around the boulder and brought the rifle to his shoulder, using the rock both as a rest and to steady the barrel as it pointed up the misty road.

Slocum wasn't prepared for what he saw next: a man stumbling along on foot, emerging out of the mists that were now rolling down from the foothills. All of the horses whickered at the sight, and began to move their hindquarters around so that they faced the man and the brisk wind. They had been facing in the opposite direction so that their rumps shielded their faces from the chilling zephyrs.

The man emerged from the rolling thick mist, stumbling, faltering, staggering. He seemed to be groping his way through the low clouds, pushed by the wind at his back, feeling his way like a drunken blind man. The wind whipped his clothing, the sound of his flapping coat startling the horses, making them nervous. He did not seem to be armed, although Slocum couldn't tell from that distance. He was carrying a cloth sack that was bulging with items inside it. As the man drew closer, Slocum saw that he was unshaven, disheveled. His trousers were torn at one knee, a gaping, ragged hole in the cloth that spread each time he stepped forward, revealing bloody, scratched skin underneath.

"Ho, the fire," the man called, his voice a loud croak that carried to where Slocum stood, then vanished in the lash of the wind. "Help."

There was an urgent pleading in the man's voice that Slocum could not ignore. He kept his rifle trained on the man and stayed behind the boulder that concealed him.

"Come on in," Slocum called. "Keep your hands where I can see them."

The man held the sack out in front of him with both hands, and picked up his pace, as if he were trying to run, but had not the strength to do more than shuffle toward the sparking fire that sent showers of glowing embers up above the rocks like a swarm of lightning bugs.

In a few minutes, the man appeared before Slocum, his face contorted with a look of desperation. He dropped his sack and stepped up to the fire, holding his hands out in front of him, palms down, directly over the flames. Slocum could see that his hands were gnarled from the cold, all twisted and misshapen, nearly frozen.

"It must be cold higher up," Slocum said, stepping up to the fire and standing to one side of the stranger.

"F-f-freezing," the man said. "God, I'm cold plumb through."

"Well, get yourself warmed up and tell me what in hell you're doin' out here in this wind, afoot, wearing clothes more fit for summer down on the flat."

The man began to rub his hands over the warming fire. He looked at Slocum, his eyes rheumy with cold and pain and the ripping claws of the wind. Slocum saw that he was shivering as his body began slowly to warm. He could almost hear the stranger's knees knocking together beneath his torn trousers.

"You got anything hot to swaller?" the man said. "Coffee, maybe?"

"Not yet," Slocum replied.

"J-j-jeez, I'm cold."

"Yeah, I can see that. You damned near said a blasphemous word."

"Huh?"

"Never mind. Get warm, and I'll make us some coffee. While I'm doing that, maybe you want to think about telling me your name and answering my question."

"What question?"

"The one about why you're wandering around here on foot, no horse, no gun, no damned sense."

The man tried to laugh, but his shivering made it sound as if he were hiccuping.

Slocum dug a sack of Arbuckle's out of his saddlebag, filled the small pot with water, and set it next to the fire atop one of the stones. He kept his eye on the stranger the whole time, and made sure his rifle was out of reach of the man, and his own right hand wasn't very far from the butt of his pistol.

When the water began to boil, Slocum grabbed a small handful of ground coffee and let it trickle into the pan. There was a faint aroma of cinnamon from the grounds. Arbuckle's always put a cinnamon stick into their coffee and there was one at the bottom of Slocum's sack.

"I've got one tin cup," Slocum said. "We'll have to take turns."

Slocum retrieved a tin cup from his saddlebags and poured it nearly full of hot coffee, careful to keep as many grounds out as possible.

The man shuffled over and took the cup from Slocum's hand. He didn't blow on it, and burned his tongue. But he took a healthy swallow and gave one last shiver as the hot liquid warmed his innards.

"My name is Ridley Corman," he said. "I was prospecting in the Tetons, panning some of the streams and rivers, diggin' around exposed roots and such. I found some color, but nothin' worth staking out a claim on. I had me a little money from a business I sold back in Louisiana and I like a game of cards now and then."

"So, you got in a card game and it turned bad on you?" Slocum asked.

Ridley squatted down and began warming his back at the fire. Slocum put more wood on the flames. Sparks shot up in the air and sputtered out in the wind.

"It was more'n that," Ridley said. "I was takin' a leak out back and overheard somethin' that I shouldn't have. When I finished up, these two jaspers saw me and when I sat back down at the card table, my next hand went bad and one of the men accused me of cheatin'. Even though I lost. I knew it was a setup, and I hightailed it out of there. But those two men drew pistols and started shootin' at me. I knew I was a dead man if I went back to the hotel to get my stuff, so I just lit a shuck. If you go into Jackson Hole, don't go to that place. There's somethin' funny goin' on there and they don't like strangers who ask questions. And make a wide path around a man named Kurt Gruber. He runs the place."

"What place would that be?" Slocum asked.

"It's a card and whiskey place called the Silvertip. Got a big old sign outside with a silvertip grizzly bear on it."

Slocum stared at Corman in stunned silence.

The Silvertip was where his friend Hovis said he worked.

2

Ridley Corman downed the rest of the coffee in the cup as Slocum stared at him, a shocked look on his face.

"What's wrong? You mad 'cause I drank all of that coffee?" Corman asked.

"No, there's more. You mentioned the Silvertip Saloon. Do you know the name of the other man you overheard? The one talking to Kurt Gruber?"

"Yeah, it was one of the faro dealers, a roughneck named Herb Duggins. Mean as a sonofabitch and if brains were powder, he wouldn't have enough to blow him to hell."

"Ever run into a man named Hovis Benton at the Silvertip? Or anywhere else?" Slocum asked.

"Hovis? Is that his name? They call him Benny there. I think he's a swamper in the saloon."

"Was he there last night when you ran off?"

"I don't rightly remember. I think so. Why? You know him?"

"Yeah," Slocum said. He wasn't going to tell Corman any more about Hovis, but from what the stranger had told him, Hovis was, if not in trouble himself, right in the middle of trouble.

"What were those two men talking about outside the saloon?" Slocum asked. "What did you overhear?"

"I don't know if I should blab it. I'm in enough trouble as it is."

"It might be worth another cup of coffee, and some vittles after that."

Slocum picked up the pan and prepared to pour. Corman sighed and scooted closer to the fire. Slocum knew what it was like to be that cold. It got into your bones and into your belly, and pretty soon it froze your brain and you couldn't think. Corman had been close to that point. He didn't have sense enough to get out of the wind and curl up like a baby in its mama's stomach to hold the heat in until the temperature turned warmer. The way he had been running, he would have gotten addled and lost his way, and frozen to death during the bone-cold night. It was dangerous to be in the mountains at night with no warmth. Corman probably didn't realize what a close call he'd had.

Corman began to shiver again. Slocum took his empty cup and set it down on the ground. The wind gusted and jiggled the cup. The tin rattled atop a cluster of pebbles. Corman looked at Slocum, a pleading in his watery eyes.

"They were talkin' 'bout a old Injun, and gold. A treasure maybe."

"What exactly did they say?"

"One of 'em, I don't remember which, said the Injun told him where there was a whole lot of gold, hidden, buried, I think, and this man said he had drawn a map. And the other'n said the Injun couldn't be trusted and he didn't believe there was any gold, and if there was, the Injun wasn't going to tell them where it was."

"Anything else?"

Corman nodded.

"Herb Duggins it was, said that they knew there was buried gold and the Injuns had stole it a long time back. Kurt Gruber, he said that the Injun wouldn't talk, even if you tortured him. Then Duggins said Kurt didn't know how to torture an Injun, but he said he did and that the Injun had talked."

"Did the Indian have a name?"

"They called him Old Eagle, once't or twice."

"Did they say what tribe?" Slocum asked.

Corman shook his head.

"I'd really like to have some more of that coffee, mister. I'm plumb froze up inside."

"When you were in Jackson Hole, did you hear any talk of hidden gold?"

"Oh, there's always talk. But, no, I didn't hear nothin' special about any treasure, 'cept when I overheard Duggins and Gruber blabbin' out back in the alley."

Slocum poured some more coffee into the tin cup. He handed it to Corman, who was shaking so badly he had a hard time getting it up to his lips. He drank all of it and then handed the cup back to Slocum. Slocum poured himself a swallow and drank it. The wind was howling through the trees and whistling through the boulders and it was even more chilling than when it had started.

"So, you don't know if the story is true?" Slocum asked.

"I dunno. It could be, I 'spose. These hills are full of stories. Some true, some hogwash."

Slocum thought differently. If Gruber and Duggins had wanted to kill Corman, there had to be something to the story about the hidden gold. There had to be a secret so big that the two men went outside in the dark to talk about an Indian who told them where to find the treasure. And if someone overheard them discussing that hidden gold, he could not be allowed to live and tell his story to someone else.

Corman, he knew then, was a marked man. He was in danger.

And he had no doubt that men were tracking Corman and meant to kill him.

"Did anyone see you leave Jackson Hole?" Slocum asked.

"I dunno. I reckon they knew I lit a shuck. But I never stopped for nothin'. Those old boys had blood in their eyes, that's for certain sure."

"So, do you think they're tracking you?"

Corman looked up at Slocum, his eyes swimming in water from the sting of the wind. He listened, cocking his head one way and then another, and the wind keened like some mournful ghost and sent shivers through him, shot fear into his heart like some dagger made of icy steel.

"Yeah, I reckon they are. Or will be by tomorry."

"And you're unarmed."

"I didn't have no chance to get my rifle or pistol. They're still in my room back there."

Slocum looked at the man and felt pity for him. He was like a hunted animal—scared, cold, unable to think straight. He was like a man looking into the very face of death, and perhaps resigning himself to his fate. Corman seemed to sag visibly as Slocum stared at him, and he wondered if Corman had already given up. He knew that animals, when injured, or aware they were about to die, would just wait and relax, go into a kind of stupor, as if they knew their death was inevitable. He had seen that same look in animals at the brink of extinction, in steel traps, mortally wounded, or cornered in a place from which there was no escape.

Slocum figured he had two choices with Corman. He could just leave him there and ride on, or he could take him down the mountain and retrace his own path later. Either way, he was taking a chance. If Corman was being pursued, his trackers would know he had stopped in this place and talked to someone, perhaps told his story about overhearing talk of hidden gold. Taking Corman down to the flats would only put them both on the run. If he left Corman here, it was only a matter of time before he was found and a bullet shot into his head.

"Can you shoot?" Slocum asked.

"I hunt for my food when I'm out in the bush."

"Pistol or rifle?"

"I'm better with a rifle."

"If you stay here, you might have to shoot a man. You might have to kill whoever's chasing you. Can you do that?"

Corman hesitated.

"I—I never kilt nobody before," Corman said.

Slocum weighed the man's words. Corman was obviously frightened, scared of losing his life. But was he also afraid of killing someone, even in self-defense? That was what separated the men from the boys. Corman had years on him, but perhaps not much wisdom.

"Ever shoot a Winchester? Or a Henry?"

Corman nodded.

"Both," he said. "I have a Yellow Boy." He paused. "Back at my digs."

"That's a heavy rifle," Slocum said. "The Winchester is lighter."

"I know."

"Well, if push comes to shove, you can have my Winchester. It's loaded. Just jack a shell into the chamber and start shooting."

"Do you think it will come to that?"

"You're the one being chased, Corman. What do you think?"

Corman went silent. But he listened to the wind, and wisps of fog, or cloud, were beginning to seep into the cracks of the boulders around them and creep along the ground like thin cotton batting, ever so slowly.

Slocum checked the Winchester and handed it to Corman. He went to his bedroll and took out the sawed-off Greener shotgun that he kept rolled up in it. He grabbed some shells from his saddlebag and put two in the shotgun, and snapped the barrel back into the receiver, where it locked. The shotshells were all double-ought buck and, at close range, would tear a man to pieces.

Besides the Colt .45 six-gun on his hip, Slocum carried a Smith & Wesson .38 tucked in back of his belt buckle, a belly gun, also a revolver, with a two-inch barrel. In his boot, he carried a concealed bowie knife, and sometimes he hung an Arkansas toothpick, a slim, deadly knife, sharp on two edges, dangling down his back. A tug on the lanyard would put such a weapon into his hands with lightning speed.

"Do you think they'll come right up on us, to where you can use that Greener?" Corman asked.

"It would be a big mistake," Slocum said.

He set the shotgun down and slipped his pistol in and out of its holster. The leather was smooth and the six-gun slid in and out like an oiled bearing slipping up and down a tube.

Corman swallowed, his eyes wide.

Slocum hadn't wanted to say anything to Corman, but for the past two minutes his senses had been prickling, and that was always a sure sign to him that something was amiss. He strained now, to listen, not to the keening of the wind, but to the sounds beneath the sounds, the sounds few people listened for, but which were often most important. In the backwoods of Calhoun County, down in his home state of Georgia, Slocum had learned to listen to those soft undertones of sound, the sound beneath sound, for it often meant that a deer was moving slowly through the forest, picking its way, avoiding twigs that would snap or leaves that would rustle.

A moment before, he had heard something off in the distance, high up on the road, muffled by the blanketing fog. He hadn't figured out what it was, but it had sounded like the scrape of iron on stone, or a horse's shod hoof. And the sound had been stealthy, isolated, inadvertent, perhaps. As he listened now, he began to hear the sounds below the wind, and they were closer, sounding like something shuffling along the road, not a man, but something bigger, like an elk, or a horse.

Then, there it was again, the ring of an iron shoe on stone. Close. Followed by the gravelly whisper of a man uttering a single word.

"Quiet."

Slocum looked at Corman and saw that he hadn't heard it. Corman opened his mouth to say something, but Slocum quickly put a finger to his lips.

Corman's eyes went wide with fright.

Slocum moved quickly. He grabbed the pan of coffee and upended it over the fire. There was a hissing sound. He stood up and began to stomp out the sparks and small flames that still lingered.

In seconds, the two men were plunged into darkness.

3

Slocum picked up the Greener. He knew that if someone was coming after Corman, they would be engaged in a close fight. It was still light enough to see, but now that his fire was out, whoever was riding toward them would not be able to see exactly where they were among the jumble of rocks.

"Stay low, Corman," Slocum warned.

"I don't hear nothin'," Corman said.

"Listen."

The sounds beneath the sounds.

Slocum strained his ears to hear what he had heard before, the muffled thud of hooves striking the ground. He knew there were at least two riders coming their way, but there could be more. And they were in a bad spot, hemmed in on three sides by huge boulders. That could also work to their advantage if the riders rode in after them full-bore.

The hoofbeats faded away into silence.

But there was something else. Slocum heard the creak

of leather under strain, as if someone were dismounting. They were very close now, he knew.

Two men emerged out of the mist. Slocum could only see them dimly as they approached. Both were afoot and carrying rifles. They wore heavy coats with fur collars. They were big men, and their hips bulged with what Slocum believed were pistols worn under their coats.

"Corman, you come out of there," one of the men said.

"We won't hurt you," the other said.

Slocum heard Corman suck in air through clenched teeth. The air made a whistling sound.

"Know them?" Slocum whispered.

"I know their voices. They work at the Silvertip. Bouncers, I think."

"Hold up there," Slocum said, as he nudged his shoulder against a boulder and brought the Greener up to his waist.

The two men halted in their tracks.

"Hey, who's there?" one of the men said.

"Lay your rifles down on the ground," Slocum said. "Then, we'll talk."

"You got to be jokin'," the man said.

Slocum snicked back both hammers of his shotgun. The clicks sounded loud in the eerie silence, as the wind seemed to abate at just that moment.

"I guess he ain't jokin'," the other man said.

"Mister, you're makin' a big mistake. It ain't you we're after. It's that lyin', thievin' thief Corman we want. He stole money from a poor widder woman and all we want to do is take him back to town and make him give the money back. We ain't goin' to hurt him none."

Slocum looked at Corman, who shook his head, a look of puzzlement on his face.

"He says he didn't steal anything," Slocum said.

"Haw. Well, then he ain't got nothin' to worry about."

Slocum could no longer keep the voices straight.

"And neither do you," Slocum said. "Just get on your horses and ride on back to town. Leave Corman be."

Too late, Slocum realized that another man, or two, was there. He heard a crunch off to his left. He turned quickly and saw a shadowy shape emerge out of the cloud bank. He squatted down, just in time, because the man fired a rifle from his hip and the bullet ricocheted off the rock just above his head, where, a moment ago, he had been standing.

Slocum whirled and squeezed off a shot from the Greener. The shotgun bucked in his hands, blasting out hot orange flame and a dozen deadly lead pellets. The shot tore through the brush, shattering tree limbs, pinecones and spruce spines. But the man had gone, in a twinkling.

The other two men opened up then, and bullets whined all around Slocum and Corman, caroming off the rocks, skidding into space with a high twang that sent shivers down both men's spines. Slocum let loose with the other barrel and heard the shot lay waste to everything in its path, everything that wasn't human. He cursed and reloaded, cracking the barrels open and, after the hulls ejected, stuffing fresh cartridges into the breech, then slamming the barrels shut.

"We've got to get the hell out of here," Slocum said, turning toward Corman.

"Ah," Corman said.

He was holding his waist and Slocum knew he had been

hit, either directly with a bullet, or with a piece of ricochet that had broken off into a leaden splinter.

Slocum muttered a curse under his breath and stepped backward to see if he could help Corman. The wounded man slumped down and leaned back against one of the boulders, still holding his side.

"I'm done for," Corman said.

"Maybe not. Just take it easy. Let me feel for your wound. It may hurt, but I want to see if the bullet went on through."

"They're goin' to get us, Slocum."

"They stand a good chance. Now shut up and let me do what I have to do."

Slocum felt around the entrance wound with practiced fingers, then traced an imaginary path around Corman's waist to his back, estimating where the exit wound might be. Corman clenched his teeth and began to groan.

"Bite down hard," Slocum said. "Think of something else besides the pain."

Slocum felt the tear in Corman's back where the bullet had ripped through. Blood poured from the hole, but he didn't feel any bone fragments. He smelled the aroma of the wounded man's intestines and knew the lead must have gone through that part of him. It was not a good sign.

"You'll have to tough it out, Corman," Slocum said. "Hold your hand back there and squeeze the skin so the bleeding will lessen or stop."

"Am I going to die?"

"Everybody's going to die, Corman."

Another gunshot and the bullet caromed off the boulder to Slocum's left. Bits of shattered rock peppered his face.

It was getting darker with every moment and Slocum couldn't see any of the shooters.

He knew that if they stayed where they were, they'd never get out alive. But he also knew that if he managed to get away, Corman would never make it. And if they both tried to run out of the rock shelter, they'd be cut down before they walked five feet. The shooters were well concealed, probably in or close to trees. They could see the rock formation and knew there was no way out except from the front. Slocum had his back against the wall, literally, and the gunmen knew it.

"Corman," Slocum said, "lie flat on your belly. Keep your head down. I'll try and get us out of here. But you've got to stick it out, no matter what."

"Slocum, I'm hurtin' real bad. Head feels real funny and I feel like I'm spinnin' around."

"Get on your belly, Corman. Real quick like."

Slocum heard a rifle cock. He ducked very low and waited for the shot to come.

Seconds later, a rifle cracked. He saw a flash, then heard the sizzle of a lead bullet as it streaked invisibly toward him. He brought the Greener up and squeezed both triggers, blasting a hole through the mist. He heard the shot rattle through the brush and strike wood, and then the solid *thunk* that sounded like one or two of the double-ought buck had struck flesh.

A man cried out as Slocum pulled his head back around the rock and clawed for two more cartridges, as he cracked the shotgun's barrels open. The empty hulls ejected and made dull *clinks* on stone. He stuffed the two shells in the chambers and brought the breech down. It locked into place with a snick of metal.

"Ow, damn it, I'm hit."

Slocum heard the man and listened for another to acknowledge him.

But there was only dead silence.

He heard a thrashing in the brush where he had fired both barrels of his shotgun. More moans and curses.

Something told Slocum to move and move fast. He stood up and was just about to run, straight for the place where he had shot one of his attackers. But then he heard a noise behind him and hesitated. The noise came from somewhere above him, on top of one of the boulders. He turned and saw a lumpy shape. He swung the Greener, but he knew he was too late. Whoever was on top of the rock launched himself in a flying leap.

The man wasn't big, but he was stocky, and Slocum felt the impact of his hard body and his weight square in his chest. The shotgun flew from his hands and whacked against a rock with a *clank,* then fell to the ground. He hit about the same time, on his back, and he fought to get away, pushing with both arms and bringing his boots up under him to push away and roll sideways.

The man drove a fist into Slocum's jaw and Slocum saw bright stars flash in his skull. He could feel the man's putrid breath on his face, a mixture of onions and boiled meat, the sour tang of beer.

"You shit," the man said, and Slocum saw his arm rise up in the air. His hand clutched a heavy pistol and he brought it down with crushing force.

Slocum barely felt the pain as the butt of the pistol

struck him on his forehead. The dancing lights in his head swirled and then were swallowed up by blackness.

Slocum sank into unconsciousness like a stone dropped into the sea.

4

The falling rain woke Slocum up as it showered on his face, cold silver needles daggering into his skin by the fierce wind out of the north.

For a long moment, after his eyes opened, he did not know where he was. Recent memory had deserted him as he had lain at the bottom of a deep ocean of sleep. He awoke shivering, darkness all around him, all landmarks invisible in the surrounding blackness. His head throbbed as if it were filled with trip hammers, pounding out a monotonous tattoo of rhythmic pain.

He sat up, rubbed his head, felt the caked blood that was already turning soft again from the rain. The noise of the falling drops spattering on the rocks made him realize where he was and it all came back to him. It was now dark, but he could see the bulky shapes of the boulders surrounding him. He looked for Corman, peering through the mist and sheets of rain. But Corman was not there and his heart sank.

Then Slocum heard something else and he quickened, and automatically reached for his pistol. He touched the grip, somewhat surprised to find that it was still in his holster. But before he could draw, the footsteps drew close, making a sloshing sound on the muddy road.

A man appeared in front of him, a rifle in his hand.

"Don't shoot," the man said. "I think I may have saved your life."

Slocum relaxed his grip on the butt of his pistol. But just a little.

"How so?" Slocum asked.

The man looked around, then stepped in among the rocks. He was dressed for cold weather, clad in a heavy buffalo-hide coat with the big fur collar upturned, a Stetson sprouting two panels of scarf covering his ears, heavy duck trousers and hob-nailed boots with flat soles.

"I come up here when I heard a lot of shooting and saw a man throw down on you. He was about to squeeze the trigger and blow your brains to cornmeal mush when I shot him with my rifle. The man staggered away and someone dragged him into the brush before I could get up to you. I figured they were lighting a shuck, so I turned to go back and get my horse, which I'd tied to a scrub juniper about a hunnert yards downslope. That's when I seen a couple of jaspers come and drag out another man who was lyin' up next to that back boulder. Figured he was one of them, so I let 'em go. I started follerin' 'em and before I knew it they were mounted and ridin' back up toward Jackson Hole, hell-bent for leather."

The man stuck out his hand toward Slocum.

"The name's Charlie," he said. "Charlie Naylor. I own a ranch near here and I was roundin' up strays. Shouldn't have come alone, of course, but I knew where my heifers were and thought I'd shoo 'em back to their mamas before the weather got any nastier."

"Slocum's my name. John Slocum. Your cattle don't winter up here?"

Naylor withdrew his hand.

"Nope. That's why we've been roundin' 'em up off the summer range. Next day or two, we'll drive 'em down to the flat, let 'em eat prairie grass through the winter. Say, what was all this about? You have a run-in with those jaspers I run off?"

"I never saw them before," Slocum said. "I'm on my way to Jackson Hole to see a friend. This prospector came walking into my camp all froze up and I was just offering him a hot cup of coffee."

"I reckon that's some of it," Naylor said, and Slocum knew he was suspicious.

He told Naylor the whole story, leaving nothing out, hoping, at the same time, that Naylor might shed further light on the situation with Corman.

"Gold," Naylor said, as he leaned against one of the boulders to get out of the brunt of the wind. "Men chase it, kill for it and cheat for it, all for what? The few prospectors I've met never found the mother lode and what little gold they did find went to the money-grubbin' merchants or wound up in the glitter houses where the fellers drank up all the whiskey they could swaller."

"You don't put any weight on a hidden cache of gold, then," Slocum said.

"Oh, there've been stories, ever since I can remember, up here."

"Any in particular that stood out?"

"Rumor was," Naylor said, "that back when this country wasn't real settled, an army patrol was escorting some miners out of the Yellowstone when they were jumped by Injuns, Cheyenne. The Cheyenne made off with the gold and the soldiers who weren't killed followed them. The Injuns supposedly buried the gold, then led the army boys into a trap and wiped them out, all except for one, who told the story down in Fort Laramie. But the boy was pretty shaken up and all that yellin' and scalpin' scrambled his brains. Nobody around here put much weight to it. You said somethin' about coffee. I smelled smoke."

"Sure," Slocum said. "I'll start a fire. I had to douse it when those men walked up on us."

In a few minutes, Slocum had a fire going again, flames licking the blackened bottom of a pan of water and ground coffee.

"I saw horses," Naylor said. "At a quick glance, they looked mighty fine. Want to sell them?"

"No, I'm taking them up to Jackson Hole. They're for a friend."

"I could use some good horses like those."

"I think my friend has need of them."

"Who's your friend?" Naylor asked.

"Hovis Benton. Know him?"

Naylor shook his head. He squatted close to the fire and Slocum saw his face clearly in the orange light. He was a man in his late thirties with close-set blue eyes, a straight nose, a square shelf of a jaw, clean-shaven, although dots of beard were starting to speckle his face. He wore an old Stetson, gray felt, crimped at the crown to suit him, a medium brim. He looked as rugged as the mountains that surrounded them.

"I don't go into Jackson much," Naylor said. "Prices are high and the merchants ain't all that friendly."

"Ever go to a saloon called the Silvertip?"

"I been there a few times. Crooked card games, loaded dice, a hangout for trail tramps and glitter gals."

"That's where my friend works," Slocum said.

Naylor shook his head, but said nothing.

"Coffee's ready," Slocum said. "Hungry?"

"Naw, I et before I rode out. Them heifers will keep for a while, though. I'm just worried about bears. Smelt a lot of scat when I rode up. They're gettin' ready to den up for the winter and if a wolf were to bring down one of them calves, well, the bears like carrion."

Slocum nodded as he poured coffee into the tin cup and offered it to Naylor. He wondered about Corman.

The two men sat on the ground and shivered by the fire.

"Tell me, Slocum, this friend of yours—what does he want with those horses?"

"I don't know."

"I could use a hand or two when we drive my herd down to the flat. Interested?"

"I might be, after I talk to Hovis."

"What about your friend? Would he help me, too?"

"I'll have to ask him."

"Is he working now? Your friend?"

"He told me he works at the Silvertip Saloon."

"Ah." Naylor sipped more coffee. Steam rose from the cup and from his mouth when he breathed. Slocum's breath was visible, too. The temperature was dropping.

"Benton might be in trouble," Slocum said. "I'm getting a funny feeling about that saloon."

"There's always trouble where they got gamblin' goin' on. But, you probably know that."

"I've heard tell," Slocum said, grinning.

"Tell you what, Slocum. I run the C Bar N. Folks in Jackson know where it is. If you and your friend can come down, say day after tomorrow, I'll hire you on for the drive down. Pay's twenty-five dollars and found. It's about all I can afford. Drive shouldn't take more'n a week. We've got some rivers to cross and some rough country until we get out of the mountains."

"That sounds more than fair, Naylor."

"My ranch lies southeast of where we are right now. I'd stay the night with you, but I want to get those calves away from the bears tonight. 'Sides, it smells mighty like snow."

Slocum raised his head and felt the wind scour his face. The air was frigid and there was a taste of snow in the air.

"Good coffee," Naylor said. "Arbuckle's?"

"Yeah. You can taste that cinnamon stick. I've got whiskey, too, if you want something a little warmer. Straight Kentucky bourbon."

"Ah, that's mighty temptin', but I think I'll go with what I got. Coffee and a warm coat."

Slocum laughed. He liked Naylor. He just might be a man to ride the river with, at that.

Naylor finished his coffee and stood up, hefting his rifle.

"Good luck up in Jackson, Slocum. I hope I see you again."

The two men shook hands. Naylor walked away, bent to the wind, straight into the mist and darkness.

Slocum put more wood on the fire and broke out his fry pan and some jerky and dried potatoes. His horses whinnied at the noise he made and at the smell of food. He would grain them before he took to his bedroll, but he wanted to get something in his belly, and take a swallow or two of whiskey before he turned in.

It began to snow and Slocum built up the fire, then dabbed a spoonful of grease in the fry pan. The wind howled in the rocks and trees and he knew he'd have to dig out his long johns before he went to bed. He cooked and ate his food, shivering in the chilling blasts of wind that circled the rocks and found him.

He thought he heard the howl of a wolf and when the horses started acting up, he knew that he had been right. A timber wolf was prowling somewhere below him and he wondered if Naylor had found his heifers and was headed home.

He cleaned his pot and fry pan and grained the horses, doling out a handful to each one, and checking their hobbles. That's when he noticed something lying on the ground near where the horses were backed up into the wind, using the spruce and fir trees for protection. He picked it up and took it back to the fire to look at it.

It was a piece of cloth that he recognized as coming from Corman's shirt. It was a large swatch with ragged edges, as if it had been sawed away with a knife. He turned it over in his hands and held it close to the firelight.

The piece of cloth was drenched in blood.

5

Slocum moved his camp that night but left the fire going, stacking it high with wood so that it would burn all night. He moved the horses, too, through the blowing snow and found a fairly dry place higher up and well off the road, where he had shelter from the trees in an outcropping of rocks.

He knew the falling snow would hide his tracks but he waited until he was sure that they had all been covered before he crawled into his bedroll and pulled spruce boughs over him, limbs that he had cut. They offered warmth, protection from the wind, shelter and concealment. He grained the horses again to keep them quiet. But it was almost midnight before he fell asleep and the snow was still falling. He hoped he would be able to get out in the morning and continue his ride up to Jackson Hole.

It stopped snowing sometime during the night and when Slocum awoke, he figured only about three or four inches had fallen. In places, the snow had drifted much higher, of course, because the wind had stayed up during the storm. He was glad to see that the horses had fared well. They had plenty of ginger in them when he saddled up and started out, switching and flicking their tails, snorting steam from rubbery nostrils and kicking up their heels like frisky colts.

The land was blanketed with ermine for as far as he could see. The high peaks of the Tetons were still shrouded in mist and clouds, but he knew they were up there, brooding over the new winter land like ancient monuments chiseled out of stone. He chewed on jerky and hardtack, drank from his canteen as he rode. He lit a cheroot when he was finished filling his stomach and the smoke bit at his throat and lungs, but warmed him in the chill of morning. The sun fought feebly to shine, but it was rising to high cloud banks far below on the plain.

He let the horses drink in the Snake River. They were thirsty and he let them slake their fill. Then he continued on toward Jackson through a snowy world of silence, the trackless road stretching out ahead of him, marked only by its lowness compared to the rest of the terrain. Finally, in the distance, he saw smoke rising from chimneys. The wind had slacked off, then vanished, and the plumes of smoke hung lazily in the air like childish scrawls on bone-white paper.

Slocum came up on a large, twin-trunked juniper, its limbs stretching out, stripped bare of branches so that it stood in stark contrast to the evergreens rising in staggered phalanxes up the mountainsides.

That's where he found Corman, hanging from a manila rope slung over one of the bare branches of the juniper tree. Corman's head hung on his shoulder, his eyes closed, his neck obviously broken. Motionless. His trouser pockets were turned inside out and he was barefoot. Somebody had stolen his boots, but left him his clothes. *What did it mean?* Slocum wondered. Were Corman's killers trying to show that he was a thief and had wound up in death with nothing? Slocum doubted that Corman had stolen so much as a crust of bread. But that would be the story in Jackson, he was sure, that a thief had been hanged, caught with the stolen items in his pockets.

Was the hanging man a warning to anyone who rode up into Jackson, or just a warning to him?

Corman's shirt was ripped and Slocum saw the slashes on his belly where the piece of torn shirt had been cut away, and there was a large gash just below his rib cage. The prospector appeared to have been tortured, but was probably still alive when they hanged him. His trousers were stained with urine and the acrid smell of it stung Slocum's nostrils. It was a grim sight and the food in Slocum's stomach roiled with swirling bile at the sickening image that dangled before him.

He clucked to his horse, Oro, and rode on, although he was tempted to cut Corman down and carry his body into town. However, he knew that would not do any good for the dead man and would put him, Slocum, at odds with the men who had killed Corman even before he had a chance to find out who they were and confront them. He wondered if the town had a city marshal or a sheriff, and if it did, would the man even give a damn?

There wasn't much to Jackson—a main street, several side streets, houses built out of lumber, stores, some with false fronts, and the usual, such as he had seen in dozens of small towns across the West: saloons, hotels, a newspaper office, a church at the end of one street, a hardware store and a mercantile that had dry goods for sale. He rode up to the Teton Hotel and was surprised at how run-down it looked, even compared to the other buildings. It was way at the end of Jackson, and beyond, he saw a building with a wooden cutout of a grizzly out front and, behind it, the sign that read: SILVERTIP SALOON, and underneath, BILLIARDS, GAMES OF CHANCE.

Between the hotel and the saloon, set back from the street in a separate field, Slocum spotted a livery stable, its large barn painted with the legend: BARNEY'S LIVERY, FEED, BOARD, GROOM. The corrals were empty and the snow around it had not been disturbed except by the wind, and small drifts had piled up around some of the posts and the woodpile. Smoke rose through the chimney at one end, white against white at cloud level.

Slocum rode toward the hitchrail in front of the hotel. He saw blurred faces behind a scummy window that was frosted over, people sitting at a table, eating lunch, he supposed, peering out at him with blank, featureless faces and eyeless, as well.

At first he wondered why the streets were so empty, and then he heard the muffled pealing of a church bell and knew that it must be a Sunday. Distant voices told him that church was just letting out and that life in Jackson would soon return to normal.

He left the horses tied together at the hitchrail and walked inside the hotel, scraping his boots on the heavy mat just inside the door. A glowing fireplace in one corner of the room warmed the lobby. He strode to the desk just as a young man scurried out of the dining room and slipped through the swinging half-door behind the counter.

"Yes, sir," the young man said, setting a ledger on the counter. "You wish to register?"

"How much?" Slocum asked.

"Uh, two dollars a night, seven dollars a week, twenty-five dollars a month. Pay in advance."

"I'll take it for two nights," Slocum said, and counted out four dollars. He would need that long just to rest up from the hard ride up into the mountains. His friend Hovis might want him to stay at Mrs. Fletcher's Boarding House, and he could do that. The clerk took his money and gave him a receipt.

"I'll stable your horses for you, sir," the clerk said. "Six bits a day for each, oats'll be a extry two bits and corn'll be free every other day."

"I'll get my gear. You know how to handle horses?"

"Yes, sir. You want to sell any of those? Horses are dear right now."

"I'll let you know."

Slocum walked back outside, stripped his saddlebags, bedroll and rifle from his horse and met the clerk coming out as he went back in. The clerk handed him a key.

"Room four, just up the stairs, Mister Slocum."

"Thanks."

Slocum crossed the lobby and climbed the stairs. He opened the door to his room and lay all of his gear on the single bed. The room was furnished, but just barely. There was a highboy dresser, on which sat a pitcher and a bowl. There was a slop jar under the bed, a table and two chairs, a wardrobe. It was chilly in the room and he was glad to see that there was a pot-bellied stove near the outside wall and a small stack of firewood a few feet from it.

He sat down and cleaned his shotgun, reloaded it, left the hammers on half-cock and leaned it against his bed. He took the Winchester out of its scabbard and leaned it next to the shotgun. He washed his hands in the bowl and dried them on a dingy towel that hung on a hook near the dresser.

Then he walked downstairs and into the dining room, which was pleasantly warm from the logs burning in a fireplace. The people who had been sitting by the window when he rode up were no longer there. In fact, the dining room was almost empty except for two men in the far corner who sat at a table drinking coffee and smoking cigars. He could see the back of one man and only partially see the face of the other. Both wore ten-gallon hats and neither turned to look at him as he entered and looked around for a table.

From long habit, Slocum picked out a place where he could sit and watch the entrance to the dining room and the men seated in the rear, who looked, even from a distance, like hardcases all cut from the same bolt. Years of traveling the West after the war, had taught him it was always best to sit with his back to a wall in any public place, and to be aware of his surroundings, which included the people he did not know and might not ever want to know real well.

A waiter near the bat-wing doors of the kitchen noticed Slocum and started to walk toward him but suddenly turned and entered the kitchen. Through one of the cloudy, smeared windows, Slocum noticed a stream of people walking toward the hotel entrance, and behind them, on the street, a procession of horse-drawn buggies and men on horseback. He figured they were coming from the church and some of them meant to stop in for lunch at the hotel.

Sure enough, people began to amble into the dining room and mingle, then separate, all seeking familiar tables, he supposed. That was when the waiter reappeared, this time carrying a slate in his hands. The waiter filed through the crowd and came up to Slocum, a fresh apron around his waist. He started to hand the slate to Slocum when a man came up behind him and snatched it out of his hands.

The waiter's jaw dropped and his eyelids peeled back as his eyes bulged and widened. He stood there, frozen with fear and bewilderment.

"You don't really want anything writ down on this here slate," the man said to Slocum. "In fact, you ain't hungry for nothin' in this town, stranger."

Slocum pulled off his heavy coat and let it hang at the back of his chair. He smoothed the black frock coat he wore underneath and stood up, facing the man with the slate, his Colt .45 bulging beneath the coat. He slid the coat open and revealed the butt of his pistol jutting from the holster.

"Mister," Slocum said, "unless you want to eat that slate, you'd better put it down on the table and be on your way."

"You threatenin' me?" the man said.

"I sure as hell am."

"You don't listen to advice none too good, stranger."

"In your case, sonny, I don't listen to it at all. Your choice. You either put that slate down or I'll open up a new hole in your belly and feed it to you."

The man hesitated. He wore a converted Remington

New Army .44, a big enough pistol, using centerfire ammunition, but he seemed to be figuring the odds. His right hand dropped slightly toward the butt of his six-gun.

Just then Slocum saw a fluttering out of the corner of his eye, a swirl of cloth, a splash of long hair and a patch of color.

The man turned as the woman grabbed his arm at the elbow and prevented him from drawing his pistol.

"Is there some misunderstanding here, Luke?" she said, staring directly into Slocum's eyes. The man she had called Luke wrenched his arm from her grasp and his hand dove like a hawk toward his pistol.

At the same time, he stepped behind the woman, putting her between him and his target, Slocum.

In that split second, Slocum made his decision. Two people might die real sudden, but he was not going to be one of them. His eyes narrowed to hard, dark slits and he went into a fighting crouch as his hand streaked like lightning toward the Colt .45 on his gunbelt.

All of the air seemed to have been sucked out of the room as the patrons froze like statues, waiting for the death roar of gunfire.

6

Slocum's hand was a blur of speed as it swept down to the grip of his Colt. He lunged forward as he drew his pistol, cocking the hammer back as it cleared the holster. The action made an ominous clicking sound. Before Luke's fingers closed around his own pistol butt, Slocum had shoved the woman aside and rammed the muzzle of his .45 into Luke's mouth.

The crowd in the dining room gave out a collective gasp.

"One twitch, Lukey," Slocum hissed, "and your brains will be all over the dining room."

"There's no need for that," the woman said. "Luke, take your hand off that gun of yours and act like a gentleman."

"This jasper was the one who was hiding out Corman," Luke said.

He was a young, hatchet-faced lout with scraggly hair that cowled his head like a dirty mop. He had close-set brown eyes that almost seemed to cross when he looked straight at someone, and his Adam's apple lay under his neck like a flint spearhead, pushing the skin out to the point of slashing through it. Luke relaxed and floated his hand away from his pistol.

"There, that's better," the woman said. She looked at Slocum. Her pale blue eyes glinted with snowy light and her lips curled up in a half-smile like some wanton Madonna stepped out of a painting into real life. "I'm Gloria Vespa," she said. "I own this hotel and I'm sorry that Luke Grissom was rude to you. But Mr. Corman stole money from my other establishment and I'm sure you didn't know anything about that when you allowed Mr. Corman to share your campfire last night." She held out a hand as if she wanted Slocum to kiss it. He ignored it.

"I don't think Corman stole anything," Slocum said. "But I see you've kept him hanging around."

Luke suppressed a smile at Slocum's macabre allusion. Gloria Vespa's smile faded like a fleeting shadow.

"Get out of here, Luke," she said. "You've done enough damage." She snatched the slate from his hand.

"But I . . ."

"Luke, get out," she snapped.

Luke slunk from the dining room. The two other men in the back joined him as he entered the lobby of the hotel.

"I should keep you around," Slocum said. "You sure know how to calm the troubled waters."

"Very funny," she said. "Why don't you put that pistol back in its holster and we'll sit down."

Slocum slid the Colt back in its holster. He and Gloria sat down. She handed him the slate. He looked at it.

"It's upside down," he said, turning it over. "Ah, at last. The bill of fare. And I see the price is dear for beefsteak."

"Everything costs more in Jackson. What's your name and what brings you here?"

"The name's John Slocum, and it's private business," he said, tight-lipped.

She sighed and turned slightly, lifted a hand and snapped her fingers.

"I'll order for you," she said.

The waiter who had brought the slate reappeared, holding a pencil and a pad.

"Bring Mr. Slocum the luncheon special," she said, "and two cups of coffee."

"Yes'm," the waiter said as he finished scribbling. He drifted away toward the kitchen.

Gloria leaned back in her chair.

"What's the luncheon special?" Slocum asked.

"Beefsteak, boiled potatoes, turnips, biscuits and a half a peach."

"Sounds good. I could eat the south end of a northbound horse."

"Tell me, Mr. Slocum, would you have shot Luke if he hadn't backed down?"

"In about one tick of a Waterbury clock," he said.

She sighed.

"I could use a man like you," she said. "Interested in a job?"

"Doing what?"

"Keeping down trouble when it arises."

"What trouble?"

"Oh, you know. Rowdy patrons, drunken cowhands, mean drunks."

"Here?" Slocum looked around, an expression of puzzlement on his face.

"No, not here. I have another establishment just up the street. It, ah, caters to a different clientele."

Slocum thought he knew what she was referring to, but he kept silent. Gloria Vespa looked to be a shrewd businesswoman and he didn't want to arouse her suspicions about his reason for coming to Jackson Hole.

"What kind of establishment would that be?" he asked.

Gloria smiled, and her pale blue eyes sparkled with light. She was an alluring beauty, Slocum thought, with her long black hair falling like rain on her comely shoulders, her patrician face and nose, her light olive skin, slender arms and legs that seemed flowing with beauty and life. Her lips were painted with just a touch of rouge, giving her an earthy, natural look. Italian descent, he thought, from her features and the olive cast to her skin.

"I own a saloon and gambling parlor," she said. "It's called the Silvertip, after the grizzly, but it's really very nice."

"I'm sure it is. I'm not a gambler, Miss Vespa."

"Please," she said, reaching over and touching the back of his hand with hers, "call me Gloria. And shall I call you John?"

"John would be all right. Gloria."

She smiled more warmly.

"You don't have to be a gambler to work for me, John. You won't be required to deal cards or handle the dice. I have men who do that for me. Professionals. We have plenty of gamblers in Jackson Hole."

"Just what would you want me to do for you?"

"Oh, odd jobs. I need a man who can wrangle horses, follow trails, read maps, lead other men. You were in the army, weren't you?"

Slocum was taken aback.

"Why do you say that?" he asked.

"Oh, just the way you carry yourself. And I detect a faint accent, southern, I'd say, but not Virginia. Farther south, Alabama, or Mississippi, perhaps."

"You're very perceptive, Gloria. Georgia. And, I was in the war. I didn't think it showed."

"I study people," she said. "In gambling, it's essential. I like to think I'm a pretty good judge of men."

"Some men are not what they seem at first glance."

"True. But over time, they reveal themselves."

"As either good or bad?"

"As what kind of men they really are," she said. "I wonder what kind of man you are, John."

"Sometimes, so do I," he said.

Gloria laughed.

A girl brought Slocum's food to him as the dining room continued to fill with churchgoers.

"Sally, why are you serving? Where's Luke?"

"He's pretty shaken up, ma'am. He got sick, so I'm taking his place."

Gloria frowned.

The girl was no more than twenty or so, Slocum figured. Twenty-one or twenty-two, maybe. She had light blonde hair, brown eyes, and the dress she wore did little to hide her figure. She caught Slocum's glance and smiled, but her eyes were agates, hard with warning. When her body blocked Gloria's as she bent over to lay his plate down, her eyes became animated, darting back and forth as if she were trying to communicate something silently. When she stood straight, the look was gone, replaced by a fixed smile.

"Will that be all?" Sally asked Slocum.

"For now. Maybe more coffee in a minute."

"Yes, Sally. Bring us more hot coffee, please."

"Yes'm." Sally sauntered off. Slocum watched her, saw her turn and beckon to him, pointing to the kitchen. Gloria missed it.

"She's a dear girl, but awkward, I'm afraid. She is not yet a trained server."

"She did all right."

"Um, yes, she did. Perhaps your presence made the difference."

Slocum dug into his food, unwilling to enter that door which Gloria had opened. He was conscious of her watching him eat and welcomed the few moments of silence she granted him. He felt her eyes on him, and knew she was studying him with interest.

"Good food," Slocum said.

Sally brought more coffee, poured their cups full. Again, she caught Slocum's glance and her eyes darted back and forth as if silently pleading for him to meet her later in the kitchen. Slocum nodded imperceptibly and hoped Gloria didn't tumble to his meaning.

After Sally left, Gloria sipped her coffee as Slocum

cleaned his plate. He sat back and drank his coffee, then fished in the inside pocket of his frock coat for a cheroot.

"Do you mind if I smoke?" he asked.

"No. Of course not." She moved an ashtray toward him. "I love a man who smokes cigars, although those appear rather small. What are they?"

"Cheroots," he said. "You don't sell them in Jackson?"

"I'm sure they have some at the mercantile store. Probably for their wealthy patrons. They look expensive."

"They're not. Just rolled-up tobacco, but I like their slimness. You can hold one in your mouth while keeping both hands free."

"Is that a gunman's choice, John?"

Slocum laughed and shook his head.

"I don't know. I was thinking about cinching up a saddle in the morning, or fixing a shoe on the trail."

"But, you have killed men, haven't you?"

"Men have tried to kill me, Gloria."

She laughed drily.

"You must play a mean hand of poker, John. You sure don't volunteer information about yourself."

Slocum didn't answer. He glanced over Gloria's shoulder. He had seen movement out of the corner of his eye. Standing in front of the kitchen door was Sally, and she was beckoning to him. He could not wave back, but he nodded a couple of times. Then Sally disappeared into the kitchen.

For a minute, Slocum wondered if he had imagined Sally being there a moment before. But, no, she had stood there, all right.

Gloria turned around quickly, as if sensing that Slocum was nodding to someone in the room.

She turned back to him, her eyes narrowing.

"Do you know somebody here?" she asked.

"Not a soul," Slocum said. "Just you."

"I'd like to get to know you better, John." She reached into her blouse and produced a ducat. She handed it to him across the table.

"Drop into the Silvertip tonight," she said. "That ticket's good for a free drink."

Slocum took the ducat and stuck it in his shirt pocket.

He puffed on the cheroot and blew a stream of gray smoke into the air.

"I might just do that," he said. "Thanks."

Her eyes flashed then, telling him that she was offering a lot more than a free drink at her saloon.

7

Slocum went to his room right after lunch, intending to go to the kitchen downstairs later, perhaps entering from the rear of the hotel where he was not as likely to be seen. He needed a bath and rest, and he was shaving when he heard the knock on his door. He wiped the lather from his face with a towel and strode, shirtless, across the room.

"Who's there?" he called out, holding his pistol in his hand and standing to one side of the door.

The knock was louder this time, but no one answered.

"If I don't know who you are, I'm not going to open the door," Slocum said.

"Please," someone said. A female voice. Whispery and low.

More knocking.

Slocum cautiously opened the door, his pistol at the ready.

To his surprise, the door burst open and a woman rushed in, a blur of cloth and hair, and flashing patent leather shoes.

It was Sally, the waitress who had served him his meal a short time before.

"Close the door," she said as she whirled to face him, her face contorted in fear, or anxiety.

Slocum closed the door and let the pistol drop to his side.

"Do you always come bursting into a man's room like this?" Slocum asked.

"Please, Mr. Slocum," she said, "I can't be caught up here and there's not much time. I had to deliver a meal to one of the rooms, which is the only reason I'm here."

"All right, Sally," he said, "maybe you'd like to tell me what's got you in such a dither that you come barging up here to talk to me. And I'm still trying to figure out what all those antics you performed at lunch really meant. Who are you, anyway?"

"My name is Sally Loving, Mr. Slocum, and I've heard a lot about you from my brother, Delbert, and from Hovis Benton."

"You know Hovis?"

"Yes, I do. And, so did my brother, Del. Oh, I wish we had time to talk. Maybe later. Could I come up to your room after I get off work?"

"Well, I probably won't be in tonight," he said.

"No, it has to be tonight. Please. Let me ask you. Did Gloria give you a chit good for a free drink at the Silvertip?"

"Yes, she did. Why?"

Sally's face fell. It seemed as if a shadow had crossed over her face, making it appear darker in the natural light of the room.

"I was afraid of that. May I see it, please?"

Slocum walked over to a chair. His shirt hung over the back. He slid out the ducat that Gloria Vespa had given him, and handed it to Sally.

"Oh, my," she exclaimed as she examined the ticket. "Oh, Mr. Slocum. You mustn't go there. Not to the Silvertip. And you must not give the bartender this chit."

She clutched the ducat to her chest as if to hold on to it.

"Better let me have that back, Sally."

She hesitated, then held it out to him.

"All right," she said, "but you mustn't use it. It will mean your death."

"What?"

Slocum looked at the ticket in his hands. The legend on it, in black, block letters, read: GOOD FOR 1 FREE WHISKEY. Underneath, there was a red image of a grizzly bear and the name of the saloon, THE SILVERTIP SALOON.

"The minute you hand that to the bartender at the Silvertip," she said, "Gloria's men will make sure you don't get out of there alive. That red grizzly bear means death."

"How do you know this?" Slocum asked.

"Don't you know who I am?" she asked.

"Yeah. Sally something. Loving?"

"Yes, I'm Sally Loving. Didn't Buddy ever talk to you about me?"

Slocum ran the name through his mind. Loving. Buddy Loving. Real name Buford Loving. The men all called him Buddy, thinking the name "Buford" was too sissified.

"You're Buddy's kid sister?"

"Yes."

"I remember him. He rode with me when I rode with Quantrill. Buddy and Hovis were good friends. Is that why Hovis came up here to Jackson Hole?"

"Yes," she said. "Buddy told me about it. He and Hovis talked about you all the time. I know the whole story of your father and brother being killed in the war, how you went back home and found the carpetbaggers stealing your home and how you killed a crooked judge and became a wanted man."

"Buddy always did talk too much," Slocum said.

Sally crumpled up and began to weep.

"They killed him," she said. "Gloria gave Buddy a free whiskey ducat like the one she gave you, and they killed him."

Slocum took her in his arms. Her hair flowed against his bare chest as she sobbed. Her hands rose and clutched his arms.

"He—he—Buddy wasn't the only one," Sally said, her voice cracking between the tears. "They're evil, Mr. Slocum, all of them. And Gloria is the devil's own temptress."

"Why was Buddy killed, Sally, and can you prove it?"

"I—I have to go, Mr. Slocum. Please. Just don't go to the Silvertip, and if you do, don't show them that ducat Gloria gave you."

She broke from him then, and scurried to the door. Before he could say anything, Sally was gone. He heard her footsteps fading as she raced down the hall. Slocum was left in silence.

He locked the door and holstered his pistol. He lit a cheroot and sat down, gazing out the window, gazing into the past.

Buddy Loving, he thought. He had almost forgotten about him. He was from Texas, he said, and he had talked about his kid sister, Sally. When General Price assigned Slocum to Quantrill, two of the men who had befriended him were Buddy and Hovis. Hovis was from Arkansas and he said he had fought at Manassas, which the Yankees called Bull Run. It had been a terrible battle, from all accounts. It seems Hovis had been visiting relatives in Georgia when he was caught up in the fervor of war and rode off with the militia to fight with the secessionists.

Slocum's father, William, had been shot and killed at that battle. He had been called up by the Georgia Militia in 1860. His brother Robert had ridden off with him, but only his brother survived the battle of Manassas.

Slocum and Robert had seen each other again in Gettysburg. John had been there when Pickett made his courageous, but foolish charge. Robert was in the leading group that charged up Little Round Top into the roar and fire of those withering Union rifles and cannon. Robert had been cut down and died, as John was with a group of sharpshooters, picking off Union troops one by one. It was a tragic day and Slocum had never felt more alone than he had when Robert had died that bloody day at Gettysburg.

He recalled that he had taken a Spencer rifle from a fallen northern soldier and used it during the battle with deadly accuracy. His aim had been true, but his marksmanship could not save his brother's life.

After that, he had become a favorite of General Robert E. Lee. But after Grant took Vicksburg, Lee assigned Slocum as a courier to General Sterling Price, a dangerous job that Slocum relished because he rode alone and did not have to watch men die every day, cut to pieces by grapeshot and cannonballs and musket or rifle fire.

The victory at Vicksburg helped give the Union control of the Mississippi Valley, and the war began to change to a different kind of fighting. At least for General Price.

"The war in the West is not conventional," Price told Slocum when he promoted him to captain. "What the Confederates lack in military prowess, they possess in marksmanship and endurance. Kansas is turning into a bloodbath."

"Bloody Kansas" they called it as Union Jayhawkers and Confederate Redlegs fought with a vengeance. The madman Quantrill had been sent in to restore order, but he had his own methods that harkened back to Genghis Khan and the Huns. His troops burned, pillaged and raped wherever they rode. Price sent Slocum to join Quantrill.

"See what makes his watch tick," Price said. "See if what he is doing is right and if it will end this war."

Slocum learned a lot from Quantrill. He learned to shoot a .45 revolver and he learned carnage that made Gettysburg look like a Sunday school picnic. But he also learned endurance and survival. And he met men, fighting men, that he would stack up against any in Lee's army. Men like Hovis and Buddy, and so many others. All crack shots, all smart, and all haters of the war they were in.

The Colt .45 became Slocum's best friend. At close quarters, the pistol had no match against other six-shooters. But in Lawrence, he was wounded and very nearly died. By the time he recovered, the war was over, and in 1866, he went back home to Calhoun County, Georgia, to another kind of horror as the carpetbaggers swarmed over the lost South like vultures, or locusts, devouring land and everything in their path.

He mused on these events once again as he bathed and dressed that afternoon. The past could never be erased, he knew. The war left indelible impressions in the minds of all who fought in it, and many believed that the issue of slavery had been replaced by another kind of servitude and an even larger injustice. Men still preyed on men, and sometimes justice came about only at the business end of a Colt .45.

"Damn you, Hovis," Slocum muttered under his breath as he left his hotel room, "what have you gotten into now?"

He headed for the boardinghouse where Hovis said he was staying.

Maybe there, he thought, he would find the answer to that question.

8

Mrs. Fletcher's Boarding House was only a stretch of the legs from the hotel. Like most of the structures in Jackson Hole, the house was built from logs, and when Slocum approached on foot he could see that it had been well cared for despite its age. The chinking was all in place and smoke spiraled upward from a brick chimney.

Slocum ascended the steps to the solid wooden porch and rapped on the door. In a moment or two it opened, and he was greeted by a pleasant woman in her forties who had but a few streaks of silver in her hair, which was drawn up in a bun. She wore an apron over a woolen green dress that clung to her figure like a glove.

"Yes, may I help you, sir?" the woman said.

"Mrs. Fletcher?"

The woman nodded.

"I'm looking for Hovis Benton, ma'am. He told me he lives here."

"He does. That is . . . he did."

"Did, ma'am?"

"I haven't seen Mr. Benton in a couple of days. What do you want with him? Are you a friend of his?"

Slocum could read the suspicion in her face. She reared her head back and eyed him as if he were something blown in off the prairie below. She cocked her head sideways and stared at him, gimlet-eyed, just the way a turkey hen looks at a garden snake.

"Yes'm, I'm his friend and he asked me to come here. Told me he was staying at your boardinghouse."

"Are you . . . ," she started to ask, then halted, changing her question. "Just who are you, sir?"

"The name's Slocum, ma'am. John Slocum."

Mrs. Fletcher breathed a sigh of relief and then seemed to relax. Her expression changed from suspicion to openness.

"Please, Mr. Slocum. Won't you come in?"

She smiled and Slocum entered the short hallway with its mirrored hat tree.

"We can talk in the sitting room," she said.

Slocum followed her into a small room that was furnished with comfortable chairs, tables, cabinets and a large sofa. The hanging beads rattled as he passed through them into the room. Mrs. Fletcher opened some drapes and flooded the room with the glaze of weak sunlight streaming through the panes.

"Have a chair, Mr. Slocum." As he sat, she went to a writing desk and pulled up the roll-top. She reached into one of the cubbyholes and pulled out an envelope. She held it clutched tightly in her hands and then sat down in a straight-backed chair that had an embroidered backrest and seat.

Mrs. Fletcher looked at Slocum a long moment before she spoke again. She laid the envelope in her lap and looked down at it, then back up. Slocum said nothing. He just watched her, wondering at her solemnity.

"Mr. Slocum," she said, "this envelope is sealed. I do not know what is in it. Paper, I gather, with writing upon it. Mr. Benton gave it to me a fortnight ago and entrusted me to keep it safe until he requested its return, or, if he was gone for more than a day without advising me of his absence, I was to give it to you."

"How long has Hovis been gone? Two days, I think you said."

"Yes. He works at the Silvertip Saloon and usually comes to his room well after midnight. When he did not return two days ago, I was apprehensive, but when he did not come home yesterday, or today, I became worried. And now you show up, almost as if we are all involved in some master plan."

Mrs. Fletcher looked toward the window and the sunlight made her eyes glisten as if she were gripped with some kind of otherworldly rapture. Slocum's skin began to prickle and the hairs stood up on the back of his neck.

"Yes'm," he said.

Mrs. Fletcher turned her head and looked at Slocum again, her gaze piercing, but her eyes still aglint, as if she had swallowed a strong drink.

She picked up the envelope in both hands and stretched her arms out toward Slocum.

"Here," she said. "Take it. That is what Mr. Benton wanted. I hope he has not met an untimely end, the dear man."

Slocum took the envelope. It was light and appeared to contain only a single sheet of paper.

"Do you think something happened to Hovis?" Slocum asked.

Mrs. Fletcher bit down on her lower lip. A frown wrinkled creases in her face. Slocum studied her face for the first time, saw the worry lines across her forehead, the smile clefts at the edges of her mouth, the coppery red hair, the bright blue eyes set wide apart, giving her an expression of both eternal wonder and, underneath, an abiding sadness.

"I—I don't know," she said, finally. "Mr. Benton was not himself of late. He—he seemed preoccupied before he gave me that envelope. He didn't say much at the few meals he took here, but I could see that something was bothering him. He didn't talk much about his work. I think he was a swamper at the saloon. But he always kept himself clean and neat. When he gave me that—that envelope, he said to give it to you in case he wasn't here when you arrived. And that's what I did. Do you think something happened to him, Mr. Slocum?"

"I don't know, ma'am. As you said, Hovis didn't talk a whole lot in one chunk. Let's see if he tells me anything more in this letter."

Slocum tore open the envelope and extracted a single sheet of paper. He recognized Hovis' scrawled penmanship, the odd spellings of words.

"John," the letter began, "if you be readun this I gess I

be ether ded or hidin out. Iffen I aint ded then I gess you will ether find me or Ill find you. You look up Sally at the Teton hotel. She be Buddy's baby sis." It was signed: "Yur good frend, Hovis."

Slocum folded the letter back up and slid it into the envelope. He slipped the envelope into the inside pocket of his frock coat.

"He may be alive, Mrs. Fletcher. I don't know."

"Does he say where he is? Where he has gone?"

"No."

Slocum didn't know if he could trust Mrs. Fletcher, even if he did know where Hovis was at the moment. She seemed nice enough, but he was still a stranger in a strange town. He did have a question for her, however.

"Mrs. Fletcher, do you know Sally Loving who works over at the Teton Hotel?"

Slocum watched her carefully as she answered.

"No, I don't believe so. I seldom go out. The boarders keep me pretty busy. Why?"

"I just wondered if she had ever come by here to see Hovis."

"No, Mr. Benton did not have any female visitors."

"He didn't have a girlfriend?"

She drew herself up as if closing off all such questions.

"I can't say. Mr. Benton and I did not discuss his private life."

"Not at all?"

"No, not at all, Mr. Slocum."

Slocum didn't detect any signs of embarrassment. Mrs. Fletcher had not blushed nor seem discomfited by his questions. Still, he wondered at her relationship with Hovis. He was a likeable man and some would say he was handsome. And he had dallied with his share of the ladies over the years. Perhaps Hovis had grown more private than he had been in his younger years.

"All right, Mrs. Fletcher. I'm staying at the Teton for two days, but I wondered if you might have a room for me. I'd rather stay here."

"I'm flattered. Yes, I do have a room. Would you like to see it?"

Slocum nodded.

She arose from her chair and beckoned for Slocum to follow her.

The long hallway stretched past several closed doors. At the last one, on the right, Mrs. Fletcher opened the door and went inside. Slocum stood next to her, a moment later, surveying the room. The walls had dowels driven into the logs, which served as places to hang clothing and other items, such as a gunbelt perhaps. There was a calendar with a Currier & Ives print on it of a woodland scene, probably in Europe. There was a neatly made bed, a dresser with a pitcher and bowl atop it on a clean doily. There was a small table and two chairs, and against another wall, a desk that was clean except for an object that sat upon it, appearing incongruous.

Slocum walked over to the desk and picked up the object, and examined it. He rattled the beads, and Mrs. Fletcher jumped as if she had been shocked.

"An abacus," Slocum said. "You don't see many of these in boarding rooms."

"Oh, my goodness," Mrs. Fletcher exclaimed, then

dashed over to Slocum and snatched the calculator from Slocum's hands.

"That shouldn't be in here. I—I must have overlooked it when I cleaned the room a week ago."

"Yours?" Slocum asked, noticing that Mrs. Fletcher put her hands behind her back, one of them holding the abacus.

"Ah, no, Mr. Slocum. It belongs, belonged, to a former boarder. A Mr. Jenkins. Wilbur Jenkins."

"Did he move out?"

Mrs. Fletcher's face drained of blood. The flesh took on an almost alabaster cast it was so white.

"Mr. Jenkins left without notice," she said tightly.

"You mean . . ."

"I mean he, uh, he just didn't show up one morning for breakfast, a month or so ago. I came into his room and saw that his bed had not been slept in. I thought he might have been called out of town. He usually came home late at night, after work."

"So, he just . . . disappeared?"

"Well, he didn't come back. I finally stored his clothing and things in the outside storehouse and cleaned his room."

"So, he disappeared. Suddenly." Slocum's tone was accusatory and his voice firm.

"Well, I suppose so, if you put it that way."

"What way would you put it?"

Mrs. Fletcher lost her composure. Her face crinkled up and she fought back tears. She brought the abacus back in front of her and looked at it. She was trembling all over, her hands shaking.

"I—I don't know what happened to Mr. Jenkins," she

said, her voice cracking. “He—he just never came home. He was an accountant.”

“Where did he work?” Slocum asked, a strong hunch growing in his mind like a snowball rolling down a steep hill.

“He—he worked at the Silvertip, that damned saloon.”

Mrs. Jenkins broke down and began to sob uncontrollably. She started to crumple and Slocum grabbed her before she fell into a swoon. Her body shook as tears flooded her face, washing away the dabs of rouge on her face.

Slocum’s jaw tightened.

The Silvertip Saloon. There it was again, looming as large as those craggy granite peaks above Jackson Hole, looming dark and dangerous, even in the harsh light of day.

9

Mrs. Fletcher regained her composure, but Slocum could see that she was badly shaken. Her first tenant's disappearance had been shocking enough, but now a second tenant was missing, and she seemed overpowered by the impact of it.

"I'm sorry, Mr. Slocum. It's just all too bewildering. I—I am just at a loss for words."

"Don't despair, Mrs. Fletcher," he said. "Maybe I can get to the bottom of all this."

"Oh, dear, I hope you can. I hope those two men are still alive."

"So do I," Slocum said, a grim expression on his face.

They walked into the front room. Slocum looked at Mrs. Fletcher, studying her tear-streaked face.

"I'd like that room, Mrs. Fletcher. I'll move in day after tomorrow, if that's all right. And you can call me John. No Mister in front of it."

"Why, that would be nice, Mr . . . ah, John. And please

call me Grace. We actually use first names here, but I always show respect for my guests when speaking of them and do not use their given names."

"Thanks, Grace. Don't worry. I'll be back."

"Good-bye, John. Thank you for coming by. You give me great comfort."

She smiled at him and Slocum smiled back.

He walked back to the hotel, the thin and melting snow crunching under his boots. The land was still flocked with white, but the sun was fighting for a foothold in the clouds and its rays were thawing many of the exposed places. Above him, the craggy peaks of the Tetons rose majestically to the sky, their granite faces covered with much heavier snow than was on the ground in Jackson Hole.

On the way back to the hotel, Slocum stopped at a small grocery store and bought jerky, hardtack and some candies. He found that they sold wine there and bought a bottle.

"Do you happen to have any Kentucky bourbon on hand?" Slocum asked.

"As a matter of fact, we do," the male clerk said. "We keep it on hand for some of our more prosperous customers, and for weddings and such."

Slocum bought a bottle of bourbon and some cheroots.

"You keep a good stock," Slocum said.

"Jackson Hole," the clerk said dryly, "crossroads of the world."

Both men laughed.

The lobby was empty when Slocum returned and he strode across it without notice. Upstairs, he entered his room. He planned to stay in that night, chew on jerky and hardtack, wash it down with wine. Although he knew he could order food sent up from the dining room, he wasn't all that hungry and he had a lot to think about. Some wine with his dry meal and some whiskey and a cheroot afterward would suffice.

He was hoping that Sally would make good on her promise to come up to his room that evening, after she got off work. He very much wanted to talk to her about Hovis and that bookkeeper, Wilbur Jenkins.

When Slocum entered his room, he was surprised to see that someone had slid a note under his door. He picked it up and locked his door, set his sack down on the floor and sat at the table to read what was written on the sheet of paper.

"John," it read, *"I hope you come to the Silvertip tonight for that free drink. I'd like to talk to you some more about that job offer."*

It was signed, *"Gloria."*

"Yeah, I bet you would," Slocum said aloud, and dropped the note on the table.

Slocum watched the dusk come on through the window, and then the land darkened into night as he puffed on a cheroot, his belly full, and the bourbon warming it. In the clear sky, the stars winked on and the minutes crawled by on a moonlit land glistening like ermine under the pale pewter light. He walked to the highboy, struck a match, and lit the lamp.

Then, the knock on Slocum's door.

He walked over to it, one hand on the butt of his pistol.

"Who is it?" he asked.

"It's me. Sally. Quick. Open the door."

She rushed in the minute the door opened and Slocum closed it. She glided through the lamplight to the window and pulled down the shade, leaving herself in soft silhouette. Slocum locked the door and walked to the center of the room.

"Any trouble getting up here?" he asked.

"No. But I don't trust Gloria. Luckily, she left early and I was able to sign my time sheet without her breathing down my neck. I left the hotel and then came in the back way. No one saw me."

"Good."

"John, I've got something important to tell you," she said.

"Sit down, then."

He pulled out a chair. Sally walked over to it and sat down. Slocum sat down in the other chair, facing her.

Sally opened her heavy coat and took out a sheet of paper and laid it on the table, atop the note from Gloria. She slid her coat onto the back of her chair. Her cheeks were still ruddy from the cold and she rubbed her hands together.

"I'm glad I'm here," she said. "I have something important for you."

Slocum looked down at the sheet of paper Sally had put on the table. He couldn't see what was on it.

"I hope it's good news," Slocum said. "I went to see Mrs. Grace Fletcher today, at the boardinghouse where Hovis was staying. Seems he's not the only boarder of hers that has disappeared."

"Hovis is alive, John," she said.

Slocum let out a long, breathy sigh.

"Do you know where he is?" Slocum asked.

"He gave me a map, but I could make no sense of it. He said to give it to you if he wasn't around."

"Did you have the map earlier today?"

"No. I had it hid outside in the alley in back of the hotel."

"When did he give you the map?"

"A week or so ago. He told me to hide it until you came to town or give it back if he was still here."

Slocum picked up the map and studied it. Then he laughed.

"What's so funny?" she asked.

"Nothing. Just a glimpse into Hovis' clever mind, that's all."

"But you can read it."

"I think so."

Sally looked down at the table. "What's this?" she said, picking up Gloria's note. "I recognize the handwriting."

"Go ahead and read it."

Sally read the note and gasped.

"Oh, the gall of that woman," she exclaimed.

"She wants me to have that free drink, I reckon."

"She wants you dead, John. She's a very dangerous woman. You stay away from that place."

"Oh, I'll get there eventually," he said. "But I'll choose the time."

She sighed and put the note back down on the table as if it were coated with poison.

"Where do you live?" Slocum asked.

"I have a place about two blocks from here, a little cabin my brother built. It seems so empty without him." She looked around the bare room, saw the whiskey bottle on the highboy. "My place isn't as bleak as this, though."

"Hotel rooms have no character," he said. "No personality."

"You're right."

"It always seems like nobody's home, even if I'm living in it. Maybe it needs a woman's touch."

"Maybe." She licked dry lips, looked up at the dresser again.

"Would you like a drink?" he asked. "Some straight Kentucky bourbon?"

"Yes. I'm still shivering inside."

"From the cold?"

"I don't know. Maybe from reading that note from Gloria. Did she hand it to you?"

Slocum got up, went to the highboy and picked up the bottle and a couple of glasses, one of which he had already used.

"No, it was slid under my door while I was gone."

"I hope you stay away from that woman."

"I'll do my best," he said, pouring whiskey into the two glasses until they were both half full.

Actually, Slocum had no intention of avoiding Gloria Vespa. He did want to meet her again, but on his own terms. She was obviously a complicated woman and such women interested him. At the same time, he knew how dangerous such a woman could be. Gloria was ambitious and accomplished. Sometimes these traits spelled poison for any man who succumbed to their charms.

Sally and Slocum drank. Slocum felt Sally's gaze on

him and knew she was studying him. It did not make him feel uncomfortable.

"You are going to see Gloria again, John, aren't you?"

"I don't see how I can avoid it. Something's been going on at her saloon, it seems to me, and it's all tied in with Hovis, not to mention others who have worked there, such as Wilbur Jenkins."

"She's a very alluring woman, John. You might wind up sparking her."

Slocum laughed.

"I have no intention of getting romantically involved with Gloria."

"Other men have said the same thing. Hovis was in love with her, you know."

"No, I didn't know."

"And, I suspect, others. Others who are no longer here. Probably no longer alive. She's like a magnet with men."

"Do I sense some jealousy here, Sally?"

She snorted in derision.

"Certainly not."

"Methinks thou doth protest too much," he chided.

"Oh, so you quote Shakespeare, too, do you?"

"He was a very wise man. Especially about women."

"And you, John? Are you wise about women?"

Slocum smiled. "Probably not."

"I wonder," she said, and in the lamplight he could see that she wore a mysterious smile, like the one on that painting, the Madonna.

"I think men and women both want the same thing," he said. "It's just that they go about getting it in different ways."

"Oh? What do you mean by that?"

"I mean there's an attraction between men and women and it's natural for them to come together at times."

"You mean to mate?"

Slocum laughed.

"Yes, I guess that's what I mean. You put it bluntly, for a girl."

Her eyes flashed.

"I'm no girl," she said. "I'm every bit the woman Gloria is, I'll have you know."

Slocum put up both hands, palms out, as if to ward her away.

"Whoa," he said. "I wasn't questioning your womanhood."

"You called me a girl," she said, scowling.

He realized he had touched a nerve.

"A mere figure of speech, Sally. You don't have to prove that to me."

"That I'm a woman?" she said quickly. "Maybe I want to prove it to you."

Their eyes locked in a steady gaze.

Slocum could feel the heat from her across the table. The heat of a woman in season.

"Maybe it's the whiskey," he said, his voice almost a squeak.

"No, John, it's not the damned whiskey. It's you."

Sally put down her glass and arose from her chair. She started gliding toward him, that same look in her eyes, the look of a woman lusting for a man.

10

Sally stood behind Slocum and slipped her arms around his neck, leaned down and brushed her lips against his left ear.

"I want you, John," she whispered and then he felt her tongue slip inside his ear. The hackles rose on the back of his neck.

"And it isn't the whiskey," she said.

Slocum said nothing. He turned in his chair and grasped her waist, pulled her to him, sat her in his lap.

"Are you sure this is what you want?" he asked, his head nestled between her breasts.

Sally heaved a great long sigh, clasped the back of his head in his hands and pulled him hard against her breasts.

"Yes," she breathed. "Oh, yes."

Slocum had not started a fire in the stove so the room was growing cold, but it mattered not to either of them. Slocum arose and guided Sally to the bed. She began to undress him and then she undressed herself. They came together naked on the bed and she began to caress him, kiss him. Slocum found her body with his hands and stroked her tummy and between her legs.

She grabbed his shaft and squeezed it, and he pried her open with his finger, releasing her musk into the air. They explored each other with their hands, their bodies golden in the glow of the lamp, the bedsprings creaking softly.

He kissed her and held her tight. Her mouth was warm and wet and her hands told him how eager she was, how willing. Her tongue shot into his mouth and he felt an electric current run through his veins and up his spine.

"I want you, John. Now."

Her voice was husky with passion, throaty with lust.

"Yes," he said. "You're ready, Sally. And so am I."

He rose above her and slid over her body. He stiffened his arms and looked down at her. She spread her legs wide to receive him and her mouth was open in a half-pout, her lips glistening with the oil of his kisses. He lowered himself and slid into her sheath.

Sally cried out with the thrill of it as he plunged deep inside the steaming cauldron of her sex. Her body bucked and her hips began to rise and fall as he plumbed her depths with his rigid cock. Her hands clutched his back and he could feel the rake of her fingernails as her body undulated beneath him.

His hard prick pried apart her lips as he swung his hips from side to side and she squirmed beneath him, exulting in the pleasure he gave her. He slid into her steaming cunt slow, then fast, and she began her own rhythmic movements until she was gasping for air and screaming softly in his ears.

"Yes, yes," she cried out and heaved her hips upward to impale him even deeper than before.

Slocum paced herself as Sally climaxed once, then twice, then another time, each orgasm more powerful than the one before. Her body was drenched in sweat and the musk of her enveloped them as the bedsprings sang and the wooden slats of the bed creaked and groaned almost in counterpoint to her own animal sounds.

"Now, now," she cooed, grasping his buttocks with both hands. "I want it all, John. I want your seed in me, every hot drop of it."

He cupped her buttocks in both hands and lifted her up to meet his driving thrusts. He went deep and fast, in and out of her cunt with rapid strokes. She gasped and gave back as hard as she got, pushing her hips upward as he came downward, faster and faster until they both reached the heights together. She screamed as he let out a long animal sigh and exploded inside her, emptying his balls in one glorious moment of triumphant ecstasy. She grasped his back with her arms and held him tightly. They rocked together on the bed as they both floated back to earth like two feathers, their bodies bathed in sweat, their hair as wet as if they had been in a rain shower.

"Oh, so good," she breathed. "So sweet."

"It was good," Slocum said, his voice husky.

Later, he lit a fire in the stove and they made love again, long after midnight. And they slept the sleep of exhaustion. Just before dawn, they came together again and she said she was amazed at his stamina.

"I hate to go home," she said.

"You don't have to, do you?"

"Yes. I have to bathe and change clothes. I hate to leave you, though."

"There's more, if you want it," he said.

"I know. You have so much to give a woman."

"I'll walk you home," he said.

"No, that wouldn't be a good idea."

"Why?"

"So far, I don't think Gloria knows that you and I are friends. But she does know that I'm Buddy's sister and that Hovis is my friend. I think she watches me. Like a hawk."

"That's a terrible way to live," Slocum said.

"I know. Life has suddenly become very complicated here in Jackson Hole. Those murders are all suspicious and I think Gloria and her henchmen are behind all of them."

"What about the law here?"

"The law? I think the sheriff is in with Gloria and her bunch. The sheriff is a joke."

"Well, we may have to do something about that," Slocum said.

"Can you decipher that strange map of Hovis'? I couldn't make any sense of it."

"I think I can find out where he is. I'll start looking tomorrow."

"You mean today, don't you?"

He laughed.

"Yes, today. First thing this morning. You take care, Sally."

"Will I—will I see you again, John?"

"I hope so. Sure."

She warmed her hands by the stove and then stood on

tiptoes and kissed Slocum. In a moment, she was gone, out into the predawn dark. Already, Slocum missed her.

Slocum put more kindling on the fire in the pot-bellied stove, carried the lamp over to the table and turned up the wick. Then he spread out the map that Sally had given him. He smiled when he looked at it again. Hovis, he thought, was plenty smart. He read the legend at the bottom of the sheet of paper, recognizing the crude scrawl. On it, Hovis had written a single word: Lawrence.

On the upper left hand corner, Hovis had drawn a compass rose, so that he knew the map was aligned with North and South, East and West.

Lawrence, Kansas. That's the town where he and Hovis, Buddy, and a number of others, had ridden into with Quantrill and his raiders. He and Hovis both knew the town well. There was a church to the north, and roads, and houses, all painstakingly drawn. But Slocum knew the scale was all wrong, and he knew why. Heavy lines marked the road to the old north church, and there was a road leading from there toward Kansas City, and it wound between other houses, oddly spaced, not in rows. He knew that each "house" was a landmark.

Hovis had drawn Lawrence, but if the map had been on transparent paper, it could have been overlaid on a map of Jackson Hole and the towering Tetons, with the Grand Teton itself standing where the old church had been.

Slocum now knew almost exactly where Hovis was holed up. All he had to do was follow the map.

The map of Lawrence wasn't Lawrence at all. It was Jackson Hole. He recognized the location of the hotel, the

Silvertip and Mrs. Fletcher's Boarding House. These were just guideposts to let Slocum know where he was now, and where he would have to go to find Hovis.

He carefully folded the map, carried it over to his frock coat and slid it into one of the inside pockets. Then he dressed as he strode around the warming stove, glancing out the window every so often to watch the night fade away. He knew it would be bone-chilling cold outside and so he put on long johns before he pulled on his trousers and slipped into a woolen shirt. He tucked his Smith & Wesson .38 belly gun behind his belt buckle, made sure his knife was snug in his boot, and then checked the Greener and the Winchester.

As the sun arose, Slocum walked out of the hotel, lugging his saddlebags and bedroll, a full canteen, and plenty of ammunition and enough hardtack and jerky to get him through this day and the next. The night clerk had not shown and Slocum left without seeing a soul. Even the streets were deserted. He walked to the quiet stables, where no one greeted him, and saddled Oro, draped on his saddlebags and tied his bedroll with the shotgun snugly placed inside. He hooked his other three horses to a lead rope and led them out of the stable. He set out for the north, the layout of the map set firmly in his mind.

He rode past dark buildings and houses, all with smoke rising from their chimneys, but without any sign of life in any of them. He had not gone far when he heard a gunshot, which startled him and Oro. The horse's ears formed into twisting cones, searching out the source of the sound. As Slocum headed in that direction, he saw a small log cabin with its windows lit from the glow of a lamp. Then he heard another shot, and another. In the bleak predawn dark, he saw two men leave the house by the back door and disappear on foot. They ran as if they were on fire, but he didn't think they were afraid of anyone in the cabin. They were fleeing, he decided, the scene of a crime.

Slocum rode up to the small cabin, jumped down from his horse and wrapped the reins around a hitchrail that stood out front. He secured the other horses to the rail. He drew his pistol and walked up to the porch, ready to shoot if he was threatened.

He stood next to the partially opened door and yelled out: "Anybody home? Hello the house."

There was no answer.

But he heard a soft moaning from somewhere inside.

"Come out," he said, "or I'm comin' in."

More moaning.

Slocum pushed the door all the way open with the toe of his boot. It slammed against a wall and stayed open.

Slocum hunched over and rushed inside the cabin. There, on the floor of the front room, lay a woman. She lay in a growing pool of blood and was barely alive.

Slocum's heart sank and he felt a twisting knife of fear in his gut.

He rushed to the woman, knelt down.

"Sally," he said.

Her eyes fluttered and then fixed on him. They were already glassing over from pain, turning cloudy as death lingered just on the edge of consciousness.

"They were after the map," she gasped.

Her eyes closed again and Slocum feared that she was dead.

His jaw tightened as he leaned down and took her head in his arms.

"Don't go yet," he whispered. "Sally, hang on."

But he knew she was dying and there wasn't a damned thing he could do about it.

11

Slocum felt blood seeping onto his hand as he cradled Sally's head in his left arm. There was no blood on her blouse, in front, so he knew that she had been shot in the back. He holstered his pistol and slid his left arm under her head, holding her gently a few inches off the floor.

"How did they know you had the map?" Slocum asked Sally.

"I—I don't know." Her voice was very weak, almost inaudible. "Saw Hovis give it to me, I think."

"Don't try to talk. Is there a hospital in Jackson Hole? Just blink your eyes twice if there is."

Sally didn't blink.

"No hospital? A doctor?"

She blinked twice.

"I'll find the doctor for you, Sally."

"Too late," she said.

Slocum fought back tears. This was no time to break down. He didn't know if there was a chance to save Sally's life, but he hoped a doctor could patch her up. She had lost a great deal of blood, he knew, and that might be an insurmountable problem. Worse than that, he didn't know where the bullet, or bullets, had lodged inside her.

"I'm going to lay your head down, Sally, and go find a doctor. Just try and take it easy."

He lay her head down. Then, to his surprise, she reached out and grabbed his hand.

"Don't go, John. Stay with me."

"You're bleeding, Sally. I'm not a doctor."

"Beautiful night," she whispered. "My last night."

Slocum's throat constricted with emotion.

"Sally, don't try to talk."

"Beautiful. Thanks. Thank you."

He felt her squeeze his hand. Then she gasped and sucked in a quick breath. Her eyes flared wide and glistened with moisture. Her gaze burned into his own eyes and her grip on his hand relaxed. She opened her mouth as if to breathe, but her chest slumped. He reached down and pushed on her chest, trying to get her lungs to fill. But Sally did not take in another breath. Instead, her eyes closed and she went silent as stone.

Slocum stood up and surveyed the room. It was a mess. Furniture had been moved around, overturned, and pictures ripped from the wall and removed from their frames. He walked through the house and it was the same in every room: the kitchen, the bedroom, the small sewing room. The two men he had seen fleeing from the house must have been inside for a long while, probably all the time Sally was working at the hotel dining room and while she was sharing his bed. His stomach turned at the wreckage the killers had left in their wake, and he tried to imagine how it must have been for Sally when she walked inside while the house was still dark.

She must have discovered the man in the back bedroom as she returned home. She had probably screamed and run to the front room where they shot her. If only he had insisted on walking her home, she might still be alive.

But the killers had not found the map. So they probably didn't know yet where Hovis was holed up, and he had to be sure none of them followed him. There was no time to waste; he knew that. Still, he hated to leave Sally like that, dead on the floor and growing cold. But he had no choice. Besides, the two killers might come back and lay siege to him inside her cabin. Or, more likely, they were waiting somewhere nearby, waiting for him to leave so that they could follow him.

Well, he had shaken pursuers before, and now, as the sky began to pale in the east, his skills would be tested again. Slocum walked out of the house and stood at the hitchrail, looking around. Nothing moved. There were no houses close by with their lamps lit, so probably none of the sleepers had heard the gunshots.

Slocum heard not a sound except the pawing of one of the horses, the whispering switching of their tails at the hitchrail.

He climbed aboard Oro and picked up the lead rope and set out from that place of death, the memory of the blood-soaked cabin, the lifeless body of Sally, still in his mind. With heavy heart, he rode slowly toward the misty peaks of the Tetons, looking around in every direction to see if he had been noticed, or if he was being followed.

He turned his attention to the map in his pocket, most of it committed to memory. He rode into the foothills on the same trail that had been clearly marked on the map. He took shelter behind a copse of spruce and juniper, stared down at his backtrail, his eyes scanning for any sign of movement. The town lay dormant in the long valley, marked by pigtails of smoke streaming from chimneys, a lamp or two glowing through darkened windows. A rooster crowed in the distance, and he heard the bark of a dog.

The thin snow on the ground was now patchy, with bare spots showing, and the clear skies promised another day of sunshine and melting. Slocum waited a good ten minutes, consulted the map again, and tucked it back into his pocket. He now knew the way, but knew he must guard against being surprised by anyone wishing to overtake him or follow him to where Hovis was hiding.

Slocum struck out again, following the trail he had seen marked on the map, but he stayed well off of it, keeping to the trees, weaving in and out, pausing every so often to look and listen. Soon, however, he could no longer see either the town or his backtrail. That's when the hackles began to prickle on the back of his neck, and he began to watch the horses, especially their ears, to see if they picked up any alien sound. It was quiet at that altitude and that far from town, and all he heard was the sound of his own breathing and the breathing of the horses as they labored up the steep incline.

The trail curved and began to weave in and out of the trees and rocks. And there were other trails leading off of the one Slocum was following. But he kept the images on the map in the forefront of his mind and figured he was still on course. He began to study the ground more closely for tracks. If Hovis had come up this way, it had been some time ago. Parts of the road were still blanketed with snow, and at those places where the ground was bare, Slocum saw no fresh tracks.

A half hour later Slocum knew he was being followed. The horses began to whicker and turn their heads, eyeing the backtrail. Slocum knew he was leaving tracks, so he rode to higher ground, well off the trail. Then he backtracked, making a semicircle, until he reached a point where he could look down at the road he had ridden.

He drew a cheroot from inside the frock coat he wore under his heavy winter coat, lit it and drew smoke into his lungs. The branches of the fir tree dissipated the smoke, blowing it uphill instead of down.

As Slocum waited, looking for signs of whoever might be following him, he had the eerie feeling that he was being watched. Such instincts had served him well in the past and he paid attention now. Was there someone nearby whom he could not see? It felt that way. Slowly, Slocum turned his head, holding the cheroot in his left hand, his right hand resting on the butt of his pistol. He looked behind him, to the right and to the left, then back down at the rutted road with its patchwork of snow.

He saw no one, but the feeling that someone was watching him persisted.

Slocum strained his ears, trying to pick up the slightest alien sound, but all he heard was the distant hawking of a mountain jay and the soft breathing of the horses.

He heard no hoofbeats, no horse's whinny, nor any sound of man or beast in that lonesome place high above the trail.

He turned Oro and nudged him in the flanks with his spurs. The three other horses followed him on a slow plod away from cover.

Slocum reined up and halted the horses. It was just a hunch, but he'd always had pretty good luck playing hunches. He pulled the Winchester from its scabbard and slid quietly out of the saddle. He wrapped his reins around a slender aspen, patted Oro on the neck and crept silently away, leaving the horses to paw at the snow for grass.

He made no sound as he circled back to where he had been, gaining still higher ground. He stopped often, behind trees, to wait, to listen. The wider circle he made encompassed the semicircle he had ridden in to check his backtrail. Now he found himself walking on flat rock outcroppings, gazing upward at stately pines and rimrock even higher up than where he was. He looked at the ground, at the branches of firs and aspen, pines, juniper and spruce, watching for anything out of place, a broken branch, a footprint, a deer or elk track, the impression of a shod hoof.

The woods seemed undisturbed. Slocum kept on, walking very quietly, stopping often, glancing at the ground and the tree branches.

He ducked under a spruce branch onto a narrow game trail. He had almost missed the trail. There, in the ragged snow and the mud left by the melt, he saw bird tracks, grouse and jays, and small animal tracks, the distinctive cloven depressions of a mule deer. The trail wound through the trees and over bedrock outcroppings until it reached another plateau on the mountainside, where it leveled off and went straight.

And that's when Slocum saw it.

His heart felt as if it had stopped.

He sucked in a breath and looked downward, his gaze finding the place where he had waited with the horses, watching the road below.

That's when he knew that someone had been watching him.

The small fine hairs on the back of Slocum's neck began to bristle and he felt a shiver course up his spine. He bent down, holding the Winchester at the ready. He studied the tracks.

Moccasins.

Indian moccasin tracks, a pair of them. Right there out in the open. They were fresh, too, the earth still steaming slightly from the heat of the man's body. Wet. Soft mud. Crushed crystals of snow.

Slocum held his breath.

The man had stood there for some time, watching him. He hadn't even bothered to hide behind a tree. He had just stood there, watching him.

Was it only a passing brave, curious, who had paused to look at him? Or . . .

Slocum stood up. He pulled down the lever of the Winchester and listened to a cartridge slide into the chamber. He turned to look over his shoulder.

That's when his heart really stopped.

He heard the same sound, but it was no echo.

Someone had just jacked a shell into the chamber of a repeating rifle.

Slocum froze, wondering when he would hear the explosion, wondering when the bullet would strike him, tearing through his flesh and crashing out his lights.

It was, he thought oddly, and fleetingly, a hell of a way to die.

12

The voice rasped on Slocum's ears.

"No move. You die."

Guttural, thick, accented, the voice was that of an Indian, Slocum was sure. And he could almost feel the bullet that was sure to come.

"It's your move," Slocum said. "You got the drop on me."

"Drop gun."

"Is it all right if I set it down? It might go off. It's cocked."

"Put gun on ground."

Slocum moved very slowly, laying the cocked Winchester at his feet. He still did not know where the man was, but he knew he was very close. Hell, he might even be looking straight at him. Indians could turn invisible, like rabbits or quail or pheasants in grass.

"Turn," the voice said. "Up hands. You go slow."

Slocum lifted both arms and turned slowly. He still couldn't see anyone, although he stared holes in the landscape in front of him.

"No move," the man said, and then stepped out into the open, a rifle in his hands.

Slocum saw an Indian wearing a coat made of buffalo fur and hide. He was short and stocky, a fur cap on his head, beaded boot moccasins, no feathers showing. No war paint either. But his black agate eyes glistened in the morning light.

"Who you?" the Indian asked.

"John Slocum."

"Why you come this way?"

"I'm looking for a friend. A man named Hovis Benton."

"Benny."

"You call him Benny. Some do, I reckon. I call him Hovis."

Slocum held his breath as the Indian studied him with those piercing black eyes.

"Hovis heap man. Me Old Eagle. Heap brave." Old Eagle pounded his own chest with a balled up fist and held his head high, his jaw jutting out proudly.

"Well, Old Eagle, if you're a friend of Hovis', he wants to see me. I brought those horses for him."

"You come Old Eagle. Bring horses. Me ride. Good."

Slocum understood the Indian. He didn't yet know what tribe he belonged to, but he was a Plains Indian. When Old Eagle turned his head slightly, Slocum saw his braids. He was probably Sioux or Cheyenne. It was just a guess.

Old Eagle gestured for Slocum to start walking. He knew then that the Indian didn't trust him, because he picked up Slocum's rifle and followed behind him. They walked down to where the horses were tied. Slocum dug out a halter from one of his saddlebags and fitted it to the trailing horse's head. Old Eagle mounted the horse in one bound, holding a rifle in each hand. Slocum marveled at his agility.

As the two men rode off, Old Eagle did something that surprised Slocum. He rode up alongside Oro and slid the Winchester into its scabbard.

"Huunh," Old Eagle grunted. "You keep."

A moment later, the Indian signed with one hand to Slocum and said, "Slocum follow Old Eagle."

The two men rode along the slope for a few minutes and then Old Eagle turned the horse he was riding and headed downslope. They crossed the road at a place where water was trickling across. Slocum noted that their tracks would be washed away almost immediately. His respect for Old Eagle rose considerably and he began to watch him more closely. He couldn't pinpoint the man's exact age, but he looked to be at least forty and maybe fifty years old or more. But he handled himself atop a horse like a much younger man.

They rode through scrub pines and junipers, a stand of stately aspen, the limbs stripped bare of the yellow leaves of autumn. They crossed another creek and then followed it for a while, again, leaving no tracks. By then, Slocum was disoriented and the drawing of the map in his mind completely useless. But he assumed Old Eagle knew what he was doing, so he said nothing.

Finally, Old Eagle began a zigzag course that took them back up across the road and to a higher level, through thick stands of trees, including fir and spruce, pine and juniper. Gone were the stately aspens, and through the tops of the trees, Slocum could see the granite faces of the Tetons, and more snow than he had seen so far, some in thick drifts, and no bare patches on the ground. They rode through a narrow canyon, which had been marked on the map, but appeared so differently that Slocum wondered if he would have been able to find it by himself.

When the two riders emerged from the canyon, Slocum saw that they were in a deep, snow-flocked meadow, surrounded by phalanxes of trees that studded the slopes up to timberline, and that mountains, lofty and snow-packed, rose high into the air. He always felt small in the Rocky Mountains and now was no exception.

Old Eagle circled the meadow, instead of crossing it, hugging the walled rim of the meadow along a narrow trail that bore only the impressions of those same boot moccasins Old Eagle wore. They rode another three hundred yards and then entered the woods where the trees were so thick that Slocum could see no more than a few yards ahead.

But the trees soon thinned and the two men entered a steep, wide canyon that was surprisingly free of heavy snow. And there, on the fringe of more trees, stood a small log cabin, tucked back into the boulders. Slocum could hear the loud gurgling of a stream somewhere ahead of them. They came to the creek where a bridge stood and crossed over it. Slocum looked back over his shoulder. The cabin offered plenty of protection. No one could attack it from the rear or either side, and anyone coming straight at it faced several obstacles, including huge boulders, the creek itself and a long stretch where they would be in the open and exposed to gunfire from the house.

A thin column of smoke rose from the chimney, and as Slocum approached he saw several cords of firewood stacked on the side of the cabin, underneath two windows. Anyone inside could reach out and grab logs from the pile without having to go out and walk in heavy snow. To the left, back in the trees, there was a protected stable, also constructed of logs, with a snow fence some yards in front of it to prevent snow from drifting too close, or inside, the shelter. Old Eagle made his way to this structure, and both men were greeted by the braying of a pair of mules.

"Where's Hovis?" Slocum asked, as they dismounted.

"In lodge," the Indian replied. "You see him soon, pretty good."

The stable reeked of the smell of corn and oats and old hay. The mules were in a stall together. While Old Eagle untied the lead rope and put up the other three horses, Slocum unsaddled Oro and put him in a separate stall. He poured oats and corn into a small trough. Oro whinnied with pleasure.

Slocum wondered why Hovis hadn't come out when they rode up. Was he hurt? Was he even in there? Who else inhabited the cabin? Questions raced through Slocum's mind as he and Old Eagle, after finishing up their chores in the stable, walked along a path to the cabin. There was no porch, but as they reached the door it opened, and there stood a man Slocum didn't know, a scowl on his face.

"Old Eagle," the man said. "Who is that with you?"

Slocum saw that the man held a pistol in his hand. His arm was outstretched, just hanging there. To Slocum he didn't look like much of a gunman. The man hadn't shaved in several days and his pale flesh was flocked with beard stubble. His white shirt was dirty beyond description, smudged with charcoal and food particles. He bore a small mustache, and even that had grown ragged. His wide forehead revealed a receding hairline, and a pair of horn-rimmed eyeglasses hung from a lanyard around his neck.

"I'm John Slocum."

"So you say."

"Is Hovis here?"

Old Eagle stood by the door, as impassive as stone.

"Maybe."

"You can be as smart-mouthed as you want, feller," Slocum said, "but I've ridden hard and a hell of a long way. Either my friend Hovis Benton is here or he's not. Which is it?"

"Let him in," a voice called out, so hoarse Slocum almost didn't recognize it. "Damn it, Wilbur, where in hell's your hospitality? That's John Slocum out there, by God, and I want to see him."

Wilbur Jenkins snorted and backed away from the door, but stood at its side, looking like a disheveled footman.

Slocum went in first, followed by Old Eagle. The room was dark except for the small fire that was nearly all coals in the fireplace. Wood was stacked up on the stone hearth next to it, but it was obvious to Slocum that they were conserving fuel. Yet the room was warm and large enough so that none in it would feel crowded. Beyond, there was a doorway with a blanket hanging from it that served as a kind of door and kept the heat from escaping.

Then Slocum glanced over in the far corner of the

room. A lamp stood on a table, with the wick turned way down so that there was only a tiny glow. Next to the small table there stood a larger one, higher off the floor. Slocum couldn't make out what was on the big table, but it appeared to be a man, and behind him, in the corner, another shape loomed that appeared to be the figure of a man standing there.

The standing man leaned down and turned up the wick on the lamp, flooding the table with light. That's when Slocum saw that a man lay there, blood covering his chest. On the floor, now that the corner was illuminated, Slocum saw several bloody cloths.

Slocum felt his heart plummet.

Nobody in the room said a word.

Slocum wondered if the man on the table was his friend Hovis. And if it was Hovis, was he dying?

Then the standing man moved again and Slocum saw something flash in the light, the blade of a knife, or a scalpel. The man bent over the man on the table and the flashing object disappeared.

Slocum swallowed hard.

The man on the table let out a guttural groan. His body twitched, and then was still. Blood spurted up in the air from somewhere and the standing man reached down and plucked a cloth from the edge of the large table.

"Is he dead?" Jenkins asked.

The standing man appeared to be tying a tourniquet around some part of the body of the man who had passed out. He wrapped it tightly, knotted it and then stuck a piece of kindling wood through the knot. He leaned down, putting his head next to the man's mouth, listening to see if he was still breathing.

Slocum's own breathing stopped, for he was sure, at that moment, that his friend Hovis had died before his very eyes.

13

Nobody moved. Nobody spoke for several seconds.

Old Eagle grunted softly in his throat.

Jenkins stood there like a frozen statue.

Slocum felt sweat ooze onto his palms until they were clammy. His stomach felt empty but swirled with a sickening roil of bile.

"John, come over here, will you, and give me a hand?"

"Hovis?"

The man behind the table stood up straight and stared at Slocum.

"Yeah, who'd you think it was? I got a wounded Crow here and I can't stop the bleeding. Bullet's in a bad spot. I almost had it."

Slocum let out a breath in a long sigh of relief and walked over to the table. He looked down at the young man lying faceup, his eyes closed. Black straight hair, buckskin shirt covered with blood, a bloody arm with a tourniquet wrapped around it. It was an Indian, his face bathed in an oily sheen of sweat.

"Glad you got here, John," Hovis Benton said. "You come at a good time."

"Where's the bullet?" Slocum asked, bending over the place where Hovis had tied the tourniquet.

"In the arm, just under the armpit. But I think it cut through an artery or something. Every time I go in to dig it out, the blood starts spurting like a damned fountain."

"What do you want me to do?" Slocum asked.

"Little Fox is out cold now. I've got to dig that bullet out and do some sewing, like those socks you and I darned in the army."

"So?"

"So, I want you to pinch off that artery while I dig the lead out, then hold it while I start sewing."

Slocum looked at Little Fox, still passed out on the table.

"He's lost a lot of blood already, hasn't he?" Slocum asked.

"Too much. But if I can get the bullet out and sew him up, we can feed him deer meat and elk so he'll grow back his blood."

Benton laughed, and so did Slocum.

"Let's do it," Slocum said.

"Put your finger right in as soon as I take off this tourniquet," Benton said. He slipped the chunk of kindling from the knot and untied it. As soon as he pulled the scrap of cloth away, Slocum put his finger down into the wound, grasped something that felt like a slippery worm and squeezed it shut.

"You got it, John," Benton said, a lilt of elation in his voice. "Now, if I can just get that hunk of lead out."

Benton dug into the wound with a slim kitchen knife. Slocum could feel the hind end of the blade against his index finger. Then he heard a faint *clink* from inside the wound. A moment later, something hard rolled up through the slash in the man's arm and Benton flicked the blade, and something black and bloody popped out and dropped to the floor with a resounding *plop*. The lead ball rolled on the wooden floor and stopped next to a table leg.

"You got something to sew that up with?" Slocum said. "I can feel that blood pumping against my finger. It wants like hell to spurt."

"Hold on, John. Wilbur, fetch me that needle and thread over yonder."

Jenkins moved fast and brought Benton a needle that was already threaded, the thread rolled up into a round ball.

"I hope Little Fox don't mind a little grease inside his arm. This thread is waxed. I done sterilized the needle in the fireplace."

"The thread looks pretty thick," Slocum said.

"It'll do," Benton said, and turned up the wick on the lamp.

Slocum's finger was beginning to ache and his hand was tiring.

Benton stuck the needle inside the wound, into a pool of blood. He fumbled around for a few seconds, then withdrew the needle. He looked up at Slocum, his face saturated with sweat, his eyes cloudy with worry.

"Too much blood in there. We need something to suck it out," Hovis said.

"Do you have anything here to do that?" Slocum asked.

Benton shook his head.

Old Eagle walked over. He leaned his rifle against the wall and made a sign with his hands to Benton.

Slocum understood what the Indian was signing.

"Let him do it, Hovis."

"Christ, why not?"

Old Eagle bent over and moved Little Fox's arm out. He put his head between his torso and arm, and placed his mouth on the open wound. He sucked the blood quickly. It sounded like a horse slurping creek water. Each time his mouth was full, Old Eagle spat blood on the floor. When he was finished, he stood up.

"You sew," he said to Benton.

"Do it quick, Hovis," Slocum said.

"Move your finger so I can get the needle in. Blood's gonna spurt like hell."

"Let me feel the needle," Slocum said. "I'll tap your fingers when you're at the right spot."

"Good. Here goes."

Benton moved the needle and thread into position very gingerly. He felt his way into the wound.

"A little more," Slocum said. "Down and to your left."

"O.K. Got it."

Benton slid the needle over. Slocum felt the end of it and curled the tip of his finger around the needle and pushed it against the artery he was holding. Benton let out a lot of thread until he had enough for a loop.

"Stick it in," Slocum said, "right off the tip of my finger."

Benton jabbed the needle downward and Slocum withdrew his finger. Blood spurted up out of the wound.

"See if there's another dry cloth, John," Benton said. "Maybe you can sop up some of the blood while I sew this wound shut. I just hope I don't block off the artery."

"That would be bad."

"I'm doing a stitch I learned from my dear mother, bless her soul. I squeezed the artery shut and am doing this by feel."

Benton kept moving the needle up and down after each stitch, running the thread through the big loop, pulling it fairly taut. He worked fast, and Slocum was amazed at his dexterity.

Slocum picked up a scrap of cloth off the table and, after each stitch, dabbed it into the wound. Soon the cloth was fully saturated with blood. He drew a handkerchief from his pocket and used that.

"There," Benton said. "I think I've got that artery sewed up. It was just a little nick, but that's all it took to make Little Fox bleed like a stuck pig. Let's see. Don't sop up any more blood, John."

Both men, and Old Eagle, looked down at the wound. Benton turned the arm over so that the wound faced downward. A small amount of blood dripped out and onto the floor, but there was no longer any spurting.

"I think that's got it," Benton said. "Now I'll sew up the wound."

He pulled the stitches tight and took a knife and cut the

thread end after knotting it several times. Then he began to sew the outer edges of the ragged wound. Again, he worked very quickly, and soon he had put in the last stitch and tightened all of them, knotted the final one and cut the thread.

"Wilbur, bring me some of that whiskey."

Jenkins got a bottle of whiskey from the top of a small cabinet and brought it over. Benton uncorked it and splashed whiskey all over the wound. Then he grabbed Slocum's handkerchief and wiped all the blood away. He splashed more whiskey onto the stitched-up wound and stepped back with a sigh of satisfaction.

"There," Benton said. "When he comes to, he may have to grit his Injun teeth, but I think the worst is over."

"Good," Old Eagle said. "Heap good."

"Why, thanks, Old Eagle."

"How did this happen?" Slocum asked.

"Well, John, let's put this whiskey to a better use than I just did and I'll tell you all about it. There's quite a story behind all of this."

"I'll bet," Slocum said.

"Let's move Little Fox to a bunk first," Benton said, "then we'll all have a pull on this 'who-hit-John.' "

"I've got some Kentucky bourbon in my saddlebags," Slocum said.

"Bring it in, for chrissakes, John. I'm getting tired of this rotgut. Not that I've had a hell of a lot of time to drink any of it. We've been pretty busy here."

Slocum returned a few minutes later with his saddlebags. He pulled out a full bottle of bourbon and Benton produced glasses.

When Old Eagle reached for one of them, Benton raised a hand.

"Not you, Old Eagle. You know what whiskey does to an Injun. Firewater bad."

The Crow looked at Benton with sad eyes.

"Want firewater," Old Eagle said.

Benton shook his head.

"Maybe when this is over."

Benton poured drinks for himself, Jenkins and Slocum. The three men touched glasses and drank, then took chairs. Slocum pulled out a handful of cheroots. Both Benton and Jenkins shook their heads, but Old Eagle took one. He and Slocum lit their cigars from the fire and sat down. The room filled with smoke.

"John, tell me what you found in Jackson Hole. I'm glad you brought horses. Ours were shot out from under us when we got Jenkins out of there. He was about to be killed. Old Eagle and his braves saved our skins with their mules, and we made it here."

"Who wants you killed and why?" Slocum asked.

"Long story, and we'll get to it. But, the skinny answer is a woman named Gloria Vespa and her bunch of cutthroats. She owns the Silvertip Saloon. Have you been there?"

Slocum shook his head.

"I met Gloria, though. First night at the Teton Hotel. She gave me a free drink chit."

"Did it have a red griz on it?" Benton asked.

Slocum nodded.

"She had you tagged right off, then. If you had presented that chit at the bar, you wouldn't have made it out of there alive."

"So I was told," Slocum said. "By Sally Loving. So I didn't go there. Not yet."

"Well, you may have to, but be on your guard. There are two men you have to look out for, in particular. That would be Kurt Gruber, who runs the saloon for Gloria, and the faro dealer, Herb Duggins. Snakes. But you'll find an ally in Ridley Corman. He's a prospector, down on his luck, who works there. He knows what's going on and is keeping an eye on things for us."

"Not any more, he isn't," Slocum said.

"What do you mean?" Benton asked.

"He's dead," Slocum said. "I met him running away from Gruber and Duggins on the ride up. They caught him though. When I rode in, Corman was hanging from a double-trunked juniper, dead as a doornail."

Benton breathed a curse and the room went silent. Slocum spewed out a plume of smoke and felt a bad taste in his mouth. He was beginning to realize that whatever was going on with his friend Hovis, it was all getting worse. And he had even more bad news for his friend. He felt as if an invisible hand was at his throat and was squeezing it tight and shutting off all the air in the room.

14

Hovis Benton and Wilbur Jenkins looked at each other, their glances dark and brooding.

"Ridley dead?" Benton croaked. "Damn."

"I was afraid that might happen," Jenkins said. "Now I wonder just how close that bitch Gloria is getting."

"Too damned close," Benton said quickly, then looked at Slocum, whose face bore an expression of puzzlement. "John, you don't understand a bit of this, do you?"

"No, Hovis, I don't. But it sounds as if you're in way over your head. What in hell is going on at the Silvertip anyway? Gambling? Cheating? Stealing?"

"There is that, yeah," Benton said. "But this situation is a hell of a lot more complicated than illegal gambling. I really don't know how to begin to lay it out for you, John."

Jenkins cleared his throat. Slocum looked at him more closely. He was a lean whip of a man with a sallow complexion beneath the beard stubble. His receding hairline made him look older than he probably was. He had a small, thin mouth and a crimped nose. He didn't look like much, Slocum thought, but such men could fool you. Many a gunslinger had made the mistake of thinking that a guy who wore glasses was a pipsqueak. But that's what Jenkins looked like, a pipsqueak, even without his glasses on.

"Why don't you just start at the beginning, Hovis," Jenkins said. "It's quite a story, you've got to admit."

Benton looked over at Old Eagle, who was absorbed with smoking the cheroot Slocum had given him. The Indian's face was impassive, but his darting glances with those black eyes let Slocum know that he was far from being asleep.

"I wish Old Eagle could speak better English, so he could tell you all this, John. But he understands a lot more English than he speaks."

"How does Old Eagle figure in all this?" Slocum asked.

Old Eagle looked at Slocum and smiled.

"Old Eagle heap smart," he said, tapping a finger to his temple.

"John, you probably didn't see them when you and Old Eagle rode up here, but right close, back behind some thick pines and spruce, there are four teepees. Old Eagle's brothers are watching over us while we sit here talking and drinking whiskey."

"No, I didn't see the teepees," Slocum said.

"Well, Old Eagle is the chief of this little band of Crow warriors and he's the reason we're having trouble with Gloria Vespa, that bitch."

Slocum puffed on his cheroot, then took another swallow of whiskey. He and Old Eagle exchanged glances. Slocum wondered what the Crow warrior was thinking.

Eagle's eyes glittered like agates in the weak firelight emanating from the hearth.

"You ever been up here before, John?" Benton asked.

Slocum shook his head.

"Well, Jackson Hole is in a long valley that leads to a place called Yellowstone. Back in '75, the government made it a national park. It's really beautiful. Know why they call it Yellowstone?"

"No," Slocum said.

"That was the Injun name for gold. Yellow stone. There's gold up in that place and Old Eagle's tribe had a heap of it. When the white man began coming up here, starting with that trapper, Jackson, the Crow moved their gold, hid it. They consider it holy, you know? Sacred.

"Well, the tribe kept moving it around, digging it up, burying it, moving on. But, as their numbers began to dwindle, they realized they had to find a place where nobody would look for it. No whites, anyways. Well, Gloria got wind of it somehow. I think one of her men saw the Injuns carrying the gold from one place to another. They shot one Crow dead and found gold on him. Then Kurt Gruber and Herb Duggins started looking for the other Injuns. They found one, Old Eagle's brother, Blue Snake, and they tortured him to find out where the damned gold was hid."

Benton paused and let out a long breath. He wiped the sweat off his forehead with the sleeve of his shirt, which was caked with blood.

Old Eagle's eyes narrowed to dark slits, as Benton continued his story.

"Blue Snake was just a young buck and he hadn't become a man yet. So these two jaspers, and probably Gloria, had a part in it, too, weaseled the location of the gold out of the boy, and then they killed him and buried his body. Me 'n Ridley saw the whole thing. Then I run into Old Eagle, grieving for his brother, wanting to know what happened to him. I told him where the boy was buried and he was mighty grateful. He dug up the body and gave it proper buryin'. And he and his band dug up the gold and moved it. Kurt and Herb were furious and Gloria had fits. Every time someone came into the saloon with dust or nuggets, Gloria's henchmen tortured them and made them disappear. Took me a while to catch on to that, though. And I got plum scared."

Jenkins spoke up, then.

"Hovis, tell Slocum what Old Eagle did."

"Oh, yeah. Old Eagle was mighty grateful that I told him about his boy and so he offered us half the gold if we could protect it and help him take revenge on Gruber and Duggins."

"And that's how you got involved," Slocum said to his friend.

"Yes, but Gruber saw me talkin' to Old Eagle, up the valley where he follered me and that's when I knew I had to make tracks. I told Wilbur and Ridley Corman about this place and said I was going to help Old Eagle move the gold to a new hiding place."

"I'm getting the picture," Slocum said.

"That Gloria, and her men, Gruber and Duggins, they've got gold fever real bad. They can smell it. They started making life hell for me and then they went after Wilbur here, threatening him. He told them he didn't know what they were talkin' about, but he knew his days at the saloon were numbered. He was Gloria's bookkeeper, you know."

"Yes, I know," Slocum said.

Jenkins got up and paced the floor in front of the hearth. He seemed agitated, like a man with something heavy on his mind. Since Hovis wasn't saying anything just then, Slocum watched Jenkins, wondering why he was upset. Abruptly, Jenkins stopped pacing. He reached down and grabbed a log and placed it on the back side of the coals, then turned around, facing Slocum.

"Greed," Jenkins said. "I never thought it could be so ugly until I got up close to it, saw it work. Yeah, I kept the books for Gloria, and until this gold business cropped up, it was a simple matter of keeping a ledger, tracking receipts, debits, credits. Simple bookkeeping. A good job. An easy job. Good pay, I thought."

Jenkins paused, and Slocum's eyebrows arched as he stared into the accountant's eyes, saw the flickering shadows in them, sensed the boiling anger beneath.

"Go on, Wilbur, tell him," Benton said.

Jenkins bit his lip, as if struggling to put his anger into words.

"Gloria asked me to set up another set of books and said they were private, not to be seen by anybody but her. When I asked her what for, she said that the Silvertip had another unexpected source of income and that was all I needed to know.

"I called this new account Vespa, because I really didn't know what it was going to be. But there were entries and disbursements shortly after that. Money would come in, in cash and gold and silver, and then there were payouts to

Kurt Gruber, Herb Duggins and Gloria Vespa. I did these disbursements by check from an account set up in my name at the bank."

"You signed the checks," Slocum said. It was not a question.

"I signed the damned checks all right," Jenkins said, a bitter tone threading his voice. "But I only filled in the amounts, not the names of the recipients. And, for the books, only initials were used. And there were some I couldn't figure out. I only knew of Duggins, Gruber and Vespa, by their initials."

"There were others on the payroll?" Slocum said.

"Two others, if I recall."

"Where did the money come from?" Slocum asked.

"Damned if I know. But it was monthly."

"John," Benton said, "maybe you can find that out for us."

"Is it important?"

"Maybe. All this started after Gloria found out about the gold the Crow have hidden. I've been puzzling over the coincidence for a hell of a long time."

Slocum glanced over at Little Fox, who was still out cold. Then he looked at Old Eagle.

"When did Little Fox get shot, Hovis? From what I heard in town, Jenkins here disappeared a few days ago."

"It happened early this morning," Benton said. "Wilbur snuck back into Jackson to try and get those extra books he made up. That was last night. The Silvertip was closed and he figured he could get in the back door and nobody would notice. He and Little Fox rode in on those two mules out there."

Jenkins broke in when Benton paused and glanced at him.

"Somebody was inside the saloon. They heard me at the back door and came out shooting. I ran and jumped back on the mule. Little Fox returned fire and got hit as we were riding away. It took us most of the night to get back here. We didn't want to be followed."

"It was a close call," Benton said. "How about you, John. Do you think you were followed?"

Slocum shook his head. "No, I don't think so. But horses leave tracks and they might be looking all over for Jenkins, and maybe me, after they find out I'm gone."

"You've got to go back, John. See what you can find out. If anyone asks you where you've been, tell them you sold those horses to me."

Slocum thought about that. He didn't know if Gloria knew that Hovis was his friend and was the reason he had come to Jackson Hole. He wanted to keep it that way. If he was going to find out anything about Vespa's sudden new source of income, he had to remain alive and well.

"That's no good, Hovis. But I think I can cover myself with the horses I brought."

"How's that?" Benton asked.

"On the ride up, the night I ran into Ridley Corman, I also met a rancher who offered me a job. I'll let it be known that I sold my horses to him."

"Who was that rancher, John?" Benton asked.

"He said his name was Charlie. Charlie Naylor."

"Oh yeah, owns the C Bar N. Good man. That might work."

Slocum stood up, stretched.

"Well, I better head on back to town," he said. "Somebody might miss me." He smiled.

"Old Eagle can guide you out of here and send you back to town a different way. Can you find this place again?"

"Yeah. I can," Slocum said.

"Good. Say, if you run into Sally Loving, tell her thanks for giving you that map. You heard about Buddy?"

"Yes. She told me." Slocum could have kicked himself. He had replied in a somber tone of voice he knew.

"How is Sally?" Benton asked, as if responding to something in Slocum's voice.

Slocum drew in a deep breath and stared deep into Benton's eyes without saying anything.

The room suddenly got very quiet.

15

Slocum struggled to find his voice. It seemed to be stuck way down in his throat. He knew the words he had to say to Hovis, but he knew they might hurt his friend. He didn't know how close Hovis and Sally had been, but he had trusted her, and, so it seemed, she had trusted him as well.

He didn't like to be the bearer of bad tidings, but there was no getting away from it. Hovis had to be told. It was just that Sally's death was going to be piled up on top of everything else that was going on, everything else that was wrong with Jackson Hole.

"Well?" Benton said, a querulous look on his face. "You had to have seen Sally. She gave you that map, didn't she? The map I knew you could figure out real quick."

"Hovis, damn it," Slocum began.

"What do mean, damn it, John? Cat got your tongue? What the hell's goin' on?"

"Hovis," Slocum said, his voice just barely above a whisper, "Sally's dead."

"Dead?"

Benton looked stunned. All of the color drained out of his face and his eyes dulled as if all the light in the room had suddenly dimmed.

"I'm sorry, Hovis," Slocum said lamely.

Benton rose to his feet. His sudden shock of grief turned to anger and he balled up both fists. He strode over to Slocum as if he meant to strike him.

"You bastard, what did you do to her?"

"I didn't get her killed if that's what you mean, Hovis."

"Killed? She was killed? Who killed her, damn you?"

Slocum was ready to block a punch if Hovis meant to fight him, but he hoped Hovis would calm down and listen to reason. Grief, he knew, could be a kind of temporary derangement, a madness that sometimes beset people when a loved one died suddenly. He wondered just how close Sally and Hovis had been. It was none of his business, but he wondered just the same.

"Sally was shot, Hovis. I—I didn't know she was in danger and I couldn't have prevented it."

"What do you mean? Who shot her? When? Why? Was it because of that damned map?"

"No one saw her give me the map," Slocum said. "But I think someone saw you give it to her."

Benton's jaw tightened and his eyes narrowed. He unballed his fists and seemed to have his anger under control. At least, Slocum thought, for the moment.

"Wha—where?"

"In her cabin, Hovis. I was just passing by. Heard the shots. Saw two men running from the place. I didn't even know that was where Sally lived."

"You—you weren't there? At her place?"

"No. I was never there. I first saw her at the hotel dining room. Just after I rode into town. Get a grip on yourself, man. They tore her place apart. Looking for something. The map, I figure. They wanted to find you. Sally just walked in on them at the wrong time."

Benton's fists doubled up again. His rage boiled to the surface. His face turned red, the veins on his neck stood out. His eyes blazed with rage.

"Damn you, John Slocum, you were always the cool-headed one. You never let any of it get to you. The blood, the torn apart bodies, the men screaming in pain, the young boys ripped apart by grape shot, the . . ."

"Take it easy, Hovis. Sally died in my arms. It gets to me. Every bit of it. I hoped she could pull through. I liked her. And she reminded me of her brother. I still don't know why he was killed. Or where. Every death gets to me, so get off my back."

Benton's eyes lost their glitter. His fists unclenched once again. He took in a deep breath and stepped back a half a pace. He looked at Slocum's hard iron face, the black straight hair that fell nearly to his wide shoulders, the square jaw, his eyes. His steady, direct, hypnotic gaze.

"Did—did she say anything? About me, I mean?"

Slocum didn't miss a beat. He didn't hesitate.

"No, Hovis. She didn't say anything. She was shot in the back. She died right after I walked in the front door. She was shot in the front room. It was very quick. I don't even think she suffered much. You know how I feel about that."

"Yeah, I do. You told me more than once that you

thought the deer you shot when you was down home never suffered none. That the shock of the bullet dulled their senses. You said it was the same with the men in battle. They all died without any bad pain if they were hit in a vital spot. I never put any shuck in any of it."

"It's true, though. I've seen too much dying not to know it's the truth."

"All right. Thanks, John. God, I can't believe Sally's gone. First Buford, poor Buddy, then her."

"It seems to me a lot more people are going to die if we don't get to the bottom of all this. I think I'd best get back to town and see what I can find out. I've got a plan. A sort of a plan, anyway. It all depends on you, Jenkins."

"Me?" Jenkins said.

Slocum picked up his saddlebags and slung them over his shoulder.

"Where do you keep those books you were talking about?" Slocum asked.

"Why, in the back room. There's an office there, where I worked. Are you going to steal them? Break in?"

"No," Slocum said. "I thought, since they need a bookkeeper, I just might offer my services."

"You're a bookkeeper?" Jenkins asked.

Slocum smiled. It was a wry smile, without mirth.

"No, but I know what numbers are. If you can just tell me how to go about it, I might be able to pass for an accountant. What kind of books did you keep?"

"I did simple double entry bookkeeping for Gloria. Debits and Credits. You put down the income in one column, the debits in another. You pay the debits out of the earnings and what you have left are credits. If you know anything about numbers, you should be able to figure it out. It's a lot of work, though. Time-consuming work. You have bar receipts, gambling receipts, supplies—which are debits—salaries. You have to make up a payroll every week."

"Sounds simple enough. I'll give it a try," Slocum said. Then, to Benton, "Hovis, you want to take a look at those horses I brought you? I've got to take a leak, so I'm going out to the stables now."

"John," Benton said, walking over to a spot by the fireplace and picking up a ten-gallon bucket, "piss in here. Piss is the best thing to clean the blood out of all these towels. We're savin' it up."

Slocum laughed and walked over. He pissed in the bucket that Benton handed him, then set it back down.

"It seems the Army taught you well, Hovis," Slocum said. "Old Eagle, I'm leaving soon. You coming to the stables with us?"

"I stay with Little Fox now," Old Eagle said. "You ready go, you come. I go with you, Slocum."

Those were the most words Slocum had heard Old Eagle speak.

"All right, Old Eagle. I won't be long. I want to get back before Gloria and her hardcases start missing me too much." Again, the slow smile that was without any humor.

The three men walked out to the stables. As Slocum saddled Oro, Benton looked over the horses, smacking his lips in satisfaction.

"These will do just fine, John," Benton said. "I'll pay you for them once we get our share of the gold. You'll get a share, too."

"We'll see," Slocum said. "So far, it's just Grandma's pie in the sky."

Benton laughed.

"Do you ever trust anyone, John?"

"Sure. I just don't wait for ships to come in that haven't even reached the harbor yet, or passed the lighthouse."

Both Benton and Jenkins laughed.

Slocum finished saddling Oro. He slung his saddlebags over the horse's rump behind the cantle and led him outside. The sun was out, scrimmed behind a layer of thin, high cirrus clouds. The snow was melting down on the flat, he knew.

"You can pay me when you can, Hovis," Slocum said. "I trust you."

Benton laughed.

"Wilbur, go and fetch Old Eagle. John, you forgot your whiskey."

"Keep the bottle, Hovis. I can get more and still have another bottle left in my saddlebags. For snakebite."

"Yeah. You and your Kentucky bourbon. You should have been a rich man by now, John."

"I am rich," Slocum said. "I just don't let it show."

Jenkins ran to the cabin, shivering in the cold. While he was gone, Benton walked Slocum and his horse over to the edge of the clearing. He stepped past some lush blue spruce and pointed beyond where he stood.

"See 'em, John?"

Slocum peered past Benton's extended hand and saw them. Four teepees in a semi-cleared place with enough trees around them so that they were both sheltered and partially concealed. Smoke rose through the smoke holes of one teepee. It was quiet.

"This is where the Crow live," Benton said. "They watch over us, in two-hour shifts. I hardly ever see them. But they're here."

"How many?"

"Counting Old Eagle and Little Fox, there are eight braves in this little village. The men are slightly past their prime, but they remember those who first hid the gold from the white man and they have devoted their lives to protecting it."

"Why?"

"They think that someday they may have to live in the white man's world, like those of their tribe who are now consigned to reservations. They want the gold to use when they can no longer hunt, and that day has long passed. All they have, really, is the gold and their old dreams of buffalo covering the land and food in every lodge."

"Are there any women here?"

"Yes. There are six women. No children, sadly enough. The women do the cooking and clean the game. We eat well, but I dread being up here all winter. Once we get snowed in, we can't get out."

"It's almost winter now," Slocum said.

"In some places up here, it's already winter." Benton looked up at the massive peaks of the Teton range and Slocum knew what he meant. He shivered involuntarily. He could imagine what a hell it would be to be caught out in the open when the first blizzard hit.

He and Benton walked back, Oro following, and by the

time they arrived at the stable, Old Eagle had a horse under bridle and stood ready to mount up and lead Slocum back to Jackson Hole via a different route.

Slocum climbed into the saddle.

"John, I have a favor to ask."

"Go ahead, Hovis."

"Would you see to it that Sally—that Sally has a proper burial? I'd give you gold for it now, but it would be a dead giveaway if you spent it in Jackson Hole."

"I'll see to it. And, it's on me, Hovis."

The two men shook hands. Old Eagle climbed on top of the horse he had ridden in on and started to lead out, riding toward the bridge.

Slocum touched a finger to the brim of his hat in a farewell salute. He wondered if he would ever see Hovis and Jenkins again.

Just then, he wouldn't have bet on it.

16

Slocum checked out of the Teton Hotel and moved into Mrs. Fletcher's Boarding House by late afternoon. He took up residence in the room previously occupied by Wilbur Jenkins. Because of what he was about to ask Grace Fletcher, he thought it was mighty appropriate to sleep in that particular room. He had questions he wanted to put to Grace, and there wasn't much time.

After he got settled in his room, Slocum found Grace in the kitchen. She was putting a stick of kindling into the firebox. A boiling pot filled with what smelled like turnips was atop the stove and the steam carried the pungent aroma throughout the house.

"Grace, may I speak with you?" Slocum asked. "If you're not too busy."

"Why, yes, John. Have a chair." She wiped her hands with a thin towel and sat down opposite him. "What is it? Are you hungry?"

"No, I ate at the hotel before I checked out. I'm fine. I

wanted to look through Wilbur Jenkins' things, those that you have stored."

"Why, whatever for?"

Slocum wondered if he should lie to Grace Fletcher or just tell her the truth. If he did tell her the reason, she might be placed in danger. He decided to lie. In fact, if he was going to assume another professional identity, he might as well get started and do it right.

"I'm an accountant, and I have need of Wilbur's abacus and some of his calculating tables."

"You're an accountant? Why, what a pleasant surprise."

"Oh? Why?"

"Mr. Jenkins, as a favor, of course, kept my books for me while he was here. And I must say that he was very neat and orderly and I surely owe him a great debt for his services."

"That brings up another matter," Slocum said. "If you want me to, Grace, I'd like to keep your books while I'm here, too."

Grace's eyes sparkled with delight. She was quite beautiful when she smiled and showed her even white teeth. And Slocum liked the way her hair fell about her face, delicate and natural, brushed to a high sheen.

"Why, that would be wonderful," she said. "I would be most grateful."

Slocum wondered if he was reading something into her tone, the emphasis she placed on the last two words out of her mouth, because it sounded as if her gratitude might know no bounds.

"Do you have his ledger?"

"Why, yes. It's in a frightful mess, I'm afraid. Since Mr. Jenkins left so suddenly, I've fallen behind in my records."

"Well, I'll try and catch you up, Grace. May I see his things now?"

She rose from her chair and led Slocum to a storeroom outside, a small building that she kept padlocked. She took a key from her apron pocket and opened the lock. It was dark inside, but everything was neatly stacked on shelves or on the wooden floor. Slocum saw that she kept the room free of cobwebs. A broom stood in one corner.

"There," she said, "on that shelf are all of Mr. Jenkins' things. I put his abacus back atop them only yesterday."

Slocum grabbed the abacus, then started looking through the packed boxes. He removed some ledgers and sheets with figures on them. He found a book of accounting principles and other items pertaining to Wilbur's profession.

"That ought to do it," he told Grace. "Thanks. When we get back inside I have another question to ask you."

Grace put the padlock back on the hasp and locked the storage building. The two went back inside. Slocum put the things he had gotten from storage in his room and then rejoined Grace in the kitchen. By then she had a coffeepot on the stove and he could smell the aroma of Arbuckle's ground coffee.

"I thought you might like some coffee," she said. "Will you be here for supper? I've got turnips and turnip greens, beef, potatoes and corn bread planned."

"Sounds mighty nice. Do you have other boarders, Grace?"

"No, not at the moment. And it will probably be this way until Spring. Oh dear, I've lost Mr. Jenkins and Mr. Benton. I was counting on that income to tide me over the long winter. The weather can get pretty harsh up here in the mountains."

"Well, maybe those two will be back before the snow flies," Slocum said, wondering if he wasn't handing out false hope to Grace.

"You think so?"

"I wouldn't count it out," he said, not wishing to divulge any further information.

"Mr. Slocum, John, I'm beginning to feel good about your becoming my newest boarder. Now, what else did you want to ask me?"

"Do you mind if I smoke?" he asked, reaching into his frock coat for a cheroot.

"No, of course not. Men smoke and if I didn't allow it, why look at how dreary my house would be."

She got up and brought Slocum a clay *cenicero,* an ash-tray that he recognized as being made in either Taos or Santa Fe. Slocum lit his cheroot and blew the smoke away from Grace's face.

"Do you know if there have been any new businesses come into Jackson Hole in the last, oh, say, six months or so?"

"Now, let me think," she said, putting an index finger to her temple. She looked off in the distance as if trying to dredge up the information Slocum had asked of her.

Slocum waited, puffing on his cheroot. The coffeepot wasn't boiling, but he could hear the water inside it begin to bubble.

"A large business," he prompted. "Or fairly large, let's say, for a place like Jackson Hole."

"Why, yes, it's odd that you brought it up, but there is one new business in town that caused quite a bit of talk. But I suppose it wouldn't have at any other time."

Slocum leaned forward over the table, his gaze intent on Grace's eyes, her expression.

"What business would that be, Grace?"

"Why, the new freight business and stagecoach line," she said. "It started up, oh, just about five or six months ago, I believe. In the spring, April or May, I think."

"What's it called?" he asked.

"Oh my, what is the name of that place? It's so new, I haven't gotten used to it. Freight something." She paused, as if riffling through a card catalog in her mind. "Grand Teton Freight Company. Yes, that's it."

"Do you know who the owner is?"

"Why no, I don't believe I do," she said. "But I remember hearing talk about why the company was started."

"That might be helpful," Slocum said, knocking an ash off his cheroot.

"There was a stage line to Cheyenne," she said. "It ran once a month, sometimes two times, during the summer. I think it was called the Wyoming Freight Line. They had stagecoaches, but sometimes a regular wagon would haul supplies up to Jackson Hole. I didn't really pay that much attention to it, but sometimes I'd see passengers get off at the Teton Hotel or the stage stop with the little café over on Spruce Street."

"What happened to that company?"

"Brigands," she said.

"Brigands?"

"Robberies. There were robberies every time the stage came up here, John. Men with kerchiefs over their faces. The company went broke, I believe, or, as some said, they got tired of being robbed every time they sent a wagon or a coach up here and just stopped coming."

"So, shortly after that, this Grand Teton outfit started up their stage line," Slocum said.

"Why, yes, I believe it was shortly after or right away. After all, we are dependent on supplies from the East and someone has to haul freight and passengers up here, and down to Cheyenne."

"Of course," Slocum said.

He mulled the information over in his mind. The events described by Grace fit a pattern. Someone started robbing the stage and made money from the thievery. Then, when the stage line quit, someone took advantage of the opportunity and started up another line.

"Has the new company had any holdups?" Slocum asked.

"Why, no, now that you mention it, I don't believe they have. At least I've not heard anything about brigands robbing the stage in quite some time."

Slocum drew a breath through his nostrils. It was beginning to make sense. Jenkins had spoken of keeping a new set of books for Gloria Vespa. A new source of income had suddenly emerged beyond the revenue from the Silvertip Saloon.

"Did you ever hear anyone say that Gloria Vespa was the owner of the new stage line?"

Grace thought about it for a moment.

"No, I don't think so."

"Well, I'll find out."

"John, what does all this mean? What are you thinking, for heaven's sakes? I don't understand."

"Anything I'd say right now would be pure speculation, Grace. But this whole business of stage holdups, and then a new company springing up so soon after Wyoming Freight folded their tent, smacks of skullduggery, or worse."

"My. That's horrible, if so. Do you think Gloria Vespa was behind the stage robberies?"

"I'm not sure," Slocum said. "If she's the owner of the new freight company, then she might have been behind the holdups."

The coffeepot was boiling now and the smell permeated the kitchen. Grace got up and moved the pot off the hot lid, and set it over the banked firebox.

"I'll let the grounds settle," she said, "and then I'll pour us some coffee. I must say your questions have set my own mind to spinning. It all sounds like some diabolical scheme, doesn't it?"

"What?"

"Well, that someone would rob the Cheyenne stage line so that it went out of business and then go ahead and take over the route for profit. What kind of a person would do such a thing?"

"That's what I intend to find out," Slocum said.

A few minutes later, Grace poured coffee into two cups. She took sugar in hers. Slocum drank his black, and he complimented Grace on the quality of her coffee, as he savored the taste of cinnamon flavor in the Arbuckle's and the warmth of the liquid as it streamed down his throat.

"I will have supper with you, Grace," he said, later. "And then I'll be out for the evening. I may not get in until very late."

"Where are you going?" she asked.

"I'm going to pay a visit to the Silvertip Saloon," he said.

"Oh, then you are a gambling man, John?"

"Maybe I am, Grace. But not with dice or cards."

From this point on, he knew, everything he did in Jackson Hole was a gamble. And the stakes were very high. The chips on the table represented life or death.

If what he was thinking was true, he was bucking up against some pretty dangerous people. And they included, right at the very top, Gloria Vespa.

17

The Silvertip Saloon & Gambling Hall was in full swing by the time Slocum arrived sometime after nine o'clock that evening.

He had walked there, since it was only a few blocks from the boardinghouse. Nearly all of the light snow had melted and the streets were muddy, but starting to freeze. There were several horses at the hitchrails out front and to the side, and the windows glowed with lamplight.

Slocum opened the door and went inside, closing the door quickly to keep out the bitter air. Only a few of the men looked up from the card tables, and none showed any interest. He waited a few seconds until his eyes became adjusted to the change of light and then walked to the end of the bar where there was an empty stool. He sat down and then slipped out of his heavy bearskin coat. He saw a line of pegs to his left and tossed it up in the air. The coat came down on a peg; a perfect throw. From inside his frock coat, he took, from a large inner pocket, the small ledger that

Grace Fletcher had given him and a stack of receipts and jottings from her files. He set these down on the bar top in front of him and took a pencil out of his shirt pocket. He opened the ledger and began to make entries.

The bartender watched Slocum for several moments before he came over, as if sizing him up. Some of the other patrons seated at the bar looked Slocum's way, perhaps wondering at his odd behavior.

"What'll it be, Gent?" the barkeep said as he glanced down at the ledger and scraps of paper.

"Straight Kentucky bourbon," Slocum said, without looking up.

"I don't know if we have any, mister."

"Then just bring me a glass of water."

The bartender snorted and put his hands on his hips in an attitude of belligerence. In the silence, Slocum could hear the snick of poker chips, the scrape of cards being dealt from some of the tables.

"Mister, you want water, go to the well. This is a whiskey bar. Beer if you want it. We don't serve water even to the horses outside."

"Straight Kentucky bourbon then."

Slocum looked up, then, and fixed the bartender with a steady stare that could melt iron.

The bartender swallowed.

"I'll be right back," he said, and scurried down the length of the bar and out through the bat-wing door at the end. He disappeared down a hall beyond the bar and Slocum continued to write figures down in the ledger. He flicked the right side of his frock coat back so that it was behind the butt of his Colt, the pistol within easy reach of his right hand.

After a couple of minutes, Slocum looked up to hear the sound of footsteps on the hardwood flooring. A man entered the back of the bar and strode toward Slocum. He came to a stop right in front of Slocum and glanced down at the papers, a scowl on his face. He was a big man, with rounded, sloping shoulders and a neck as thick as cordwood, small porcine eyes buried behind satchels of puffy fat.

"Our whiskey ain't good enough for you, stranger?" the man said.

"I wouldn't know," Slocum said. "I never tasted it. Are you offering me a sample?"

"Sample, my ass. Do you have a free drink chit?"

"Grace Vespa gave me one, but I lost it."

"Then, no free drinks, bud. No free samples. Now, what will you have? Beer or whiskey?"

"Whiskey. Straight Kentucky bourbon."

"We've got Old Taylor. That good enough?"

"Good enough," Slocum said.

"I'll get the barkeep. What's that stuff you're doing there?"

"Oh, work for a friend," Slocum said affably.

"My advice. Do that stuff at home, bud. This is a saloon. You can drink and you can gamble. That's about it."

"I work better in a nice saloon such as this. Bud."

The beefy man scowled, but said nothing. In another few moments, the bartender returned. He brought a bottle and a shot glass over to Slocum. He poured the glass full and set the bottle down on the bartop.

"That'll be six bits," the barkeep said.

Slocum laid out a dollar.

"Keep the change," he said.

The bartender swept up the bill, but didn't reply. He took the bottle with him, as if he didn't trust Slocum with it.

Slocum took a sip of whiskey and turned on the stool to look at the other patrons, the dealers. The saloon was a large log building, solidly built. There was a mirror behind the bar, with rows of bottles stacked in front of it. There was a beer dispenser attached to a keg beneath the bar top. Men sat at tables playing cards and there was a craps table in the center of the room. Two or three men were betting on the dice. There was also a faro dealer in the back corner, wearing an eyeshade. He had delicate hands, and fingers so slender they might have belonged to a woman. Cigar and cigarette smoke hung in the air. The lamps on the wall were backed by small mirrors which threw out light in a high intensity spray. A chandelier with candles made sure that there were few shadows cast in the room and none on any of the gaming tables.

Along the back wall, facing the room, there was a large panel of smoked glass. Slocum could picture in his mind what was behind it, a small dark room where men could sit and look out at all the gaming tables. Such watchers could detect trouble and take appropriate action. Gloria had thought of just about everything when she designed her saloon.

He thought Gloria might still be at the hotel dining room, perhaps closing up for the evening so that she could attend to her saloon business. The woman was seemingly into everything, so he figured she was smart and capable, perhaps a very good businesswoman. Most men thought women belonged in the home, not in the world of commerce, but Slocum had, over the years, come across many capable women, even some who outstripped the men in business acumen. So far, Gloria seemed to be one of these women; smart, capable, and hard-nosed in business.

He lit a cheroot, polished off the shot of whiskey and held up a finger in a sign to the barkeep that he wanted another. He laid a silver dollar on the bar top, slapping it down so that it made a sound. The bartender looked his way and came over with the bottle. He poured the shot glass full with an expert hand and scooped up the silver dollar. He didn't bother to wipe the bar with his towel, but gave Slocum a look of utter contempt.

"Be careful, Shorty," Slocum said, "you might have to wear that look to your grave."

"What's that? You callin' me out, Mister?"

"Listen, if I was calling you out, Slim, we'd already be at the ball."

"You've got a smart mouth, Mister."

"I'll take that as a compliment," Slocum said. "Oh, and you can keep the change. I figure two bits is about all you're worth."

The bartender drew himself up with a look of indignation, snatched the bottle of Old Taylor off the counter and walked back to the other end of the bar where he had been carrying on a conversation. Slocum blew a plume of smoke in his direction and the man turned his head.

A man sitting on a stool nearby, his red cheeks beaming beneath his grizzled gray and black beard, turned to Slocum.

"This ain't no good place for a man to make enemies, Pilgrim."

"No place is."

"You may not want no advice, stranger, but you done rubbed at least two people the wrong way, Freddie Hewitt, the barkeep, and Herb Duggins, the bouncer."

"Oh, I wondered who that was. Herb Duggins, eh?"

"He's a hard one," the old galoot said, "almost as hard as another jasper who works here, Kurt Gruber. You don't want to run up against him. Not if you want to keep all your teeth in your head."

"I'll keep that in mind," Slocum said. "Thanks for the advice."

"The name's Cooley. Jocko Cooley."

"You don't gamble, I take it."

"I learned that lesson a long time ago. Somethin' like a fool and his money are soon parted. Nope. I just drink. Keeps these old bones fluid, you know."

Slocum laughed.

"I'm John Slocum."

"You're new in town. And I hope you have a friend or two outside of the Silvertip, 'cause you sure ain't makin' none here. 'Cept for me, that is, and I may be doubtful."

Slocum laughed again.

"No, I don't have any friends here. But I appreciate meeting you, Jocko."

"Same here, Slocum."

Slocum lifted his drink glass in a silent toast to Jocko and sipped half of it. He heard a door open somewhere in back, down at the end of that dark hall where Herb Duggins had disappeared. He could not see into the darkness, but he heard footsteps, and then another door opened and slammed shut. After that, he looked over at the smoked glass and felt as if someone were watching him. He smoked and listened to the drone of conversation in the room, then turned back to the ledger and began making entries in the debit column.

He didn't see her when she came up, she was so quiet. But he smelled the heady aroma of her perfume.

"Good evening, Mr. Slocum," Gloria said. "Welcome to the Silvertip."

Slocum turned and looked at Gloria Vespa. She nearly took his breath away. In the glow of the candles overhead, her black hair shone like a crow's wing in the sunlight. She was wearing a dark blue dress with the bodice cut very low so that the tops of her breasts protruded like a pair of ripe honeydew melons. The bodice was rimmed with intricate lace, as were the sleeves and hem of her dress. She wore a bright red ribbon in her hair that highlighted the band of ribbon above the hem of her dress and the bands encircling her sleeves.

"Hello, Gloria. I wondered when you would show up."

"I just got in. We had a busy night at the hotel. I half expected you to drop in for supper."

"I moved into a boardinghouse. Had supper there."

"Mrs. Fletcher's?"

"Yes. Do you know her?"

"No, but some of my employees have stayed there. They speak very highly of her cooking. What have you got there?" She pointed to the ledger and the pile of papers.

"Oh, I'm bringing Grace Fletcher's books up to date. Seems her regular bookkeeper moved out all of a sudden."

"You're a bookkeeper?" she said, in a tone that was almost mocking in its hint of incredulity.

"Yeah, I'm a certified accountant."

"You don't look like any bookkeeper I ever saw."

"Well, we come in all sizes and shapes, Gloria."

She laughed.

"I want to talk to you, then, John. Did you get your free drink? I gave you a ducat, you know."

"No, ma'am. I guess I lost it."

She sat down on the stool next to Slocum and looked directly into his eyes.

"Well, we'll just have to correct that mistake, won't we?"

"You're going to give me another chit?" he said.

She licked her luscious painted lips, flicking her tongue over them like a serpent's. She gazed deep into Slocum's eyes and he felt the tiniest of shivers run up his spine, as if a black widow spider had just crawled up his back and was about to bite him in the neck.

18

Slocum didn't avert his gaze. Nor did Gloria. The two stared at each other like a pair of gunfighters squaring off for a fight. But she had asked him a question and she deserved a reply.

"No, Gloria. I'd probably lose that free drink ticket before I even got a chance to use it. Besides, I can pay for my own drinks."

"Oh, you don't need a ducat to get a free drink tonight, John. I'll buy the next one. And I hope you will take me up on my offer because I'd like to talk business with you."

"You offered me a job, Gloria. But I'm no gambler. And I don't think I'd make a good bouncer."

"What if I offered to buy your gun?" she asked, still keeping that steady gaze on Slocum.

"Naw, I'm not much good for that, either. I use my pistol for a hammer, mostly, in case my horse throws a shoe."

Again, as she had at the hotel, she eyed him up and down, as if to reassess her judgment.

"I can hardly believe that," she said. "You have the look of a man who knows the business end of a Colt."

"Oh, I never use that end. Like I said . . ."

"I know. You use that gun on your belt for a hammer."

"Yes'm," he said meekly, and smiled disarmingly.

"Let me take a look at those books you're doing for Mrs. Fletcher," she said.

Slocum slid the ledger and receipts over to her. She looked at his entries and at the scraps of paper. Satisfied, she pushed them back.

"Find any numbers there that caught your fancy?" Slocum teased.

"You write neat figures," she said. "I still don't know if you can add or subtract."

"Test me," he said.

"Some other time, perhaps. So, you're a bookkeeper. Interested in a job? Working for me?"

"I might be. I'm just doing this as a favor to Mrs. Fletcher."

"I wonder what other favors she'll want you to do for her, John."

Slocum thought it wise to stay silent.

"Now, that wasn't very nice of me, was it? I don't even know the woman. But she obviously trusts you to do her books, so I'll take that as a recommendation."

"Yes'm," Slocum said, playing the slow dunce.

"Will you come to work for me, then? I can pay you fifty dollars a month. Will that be all right?"

"Sixty," Slocum said. "And free drinks when I'm not working."

"You drive a hard bargain, John. You don't look like

much of a businessman, but perhaps you are. Sixty a month and two free drinks every night of the week except Saturday. How's that?"

"Will tonight's free drink count against my salary?"

Gloria laughed.

"No, of course not. Can you start tomorrow?"

"Tomorrow afternoon," he said. "After lunch."

"Fair enough. I'll take time away from the dining room to explain the ins and outs of the job for you."

"That would be helpful," Slocum said, drawing on his cheroot. He blew the smoke toward the wall, where it flattened and dissipated.

"I'll look for you tomorrow afternoon around one," she said. Then she reached over and laid her hand atop Slocum's. She patted it, then gave it a little squeeze. "I'm looking forward to working with you, John. I think we might have a beautiful relationship."

"Me, too, ma'am."

"Will you please call me Gloria? We're not very formal around here, but 'ma'am' makes me feel old."

"I'm sorry. You sure aren't old, Gloria. I was just being polite."

"And, that's another thing I like about you, Mr. Slocum. You are polite, and you appear to have good manners, at least with the ladies."

"Yes'm," he said, feeling like the dolt he was trying to portray.

"I also think you're a lot deeper than you look. Still waters and all."

He started to say "Yes'm" again, but thought better of it. He didn't want to push too much. He had the job of bookkeeper and that's what he had come there for. And he knew he had a busy morning coming up. He finished his drink and Gloria smiled.

"Ready for one on the house?" she said.

"Sure. Then that's my limit. I'm not yet settled in and I'd like to get a good night's sleep without too much of a swollen head."

She laughed and snapped her fingers at Freddie Hewitt, the bartender. She pointed to Slocum's empty glass and he brought the bottle of Old Taylor over.

"I'm buying Mr. Slocum this drink, Freddie," she said. "Pour it generous."

"I always do, Gloria. That's your rule."

Hewitt poured Slocum's glass full and started to take the bottle away.

"I think I'd like a drink, too, Freddie. Just a taste. Mr. Slocum is going to work for me. Starting tomorrow. And every night, after work, except on Saturday nights, he gets two free drinks, just like you and everybody else who works here."

Slocum's eyebrows arched.

Gloria smiled knowingly at him.

Hewitt poured a snifter half full and set it before Gloria, then picked up the bottle to take it back down to the other end of the bar.

"Hold on, Hewitt," Slocum said. "I'd like to buy Jocko Cooley over there a drink." He pointed toward the old prospector and put another silver dollar on the bar. "Jocko, will you have a drink on me?"

Jocko nodded and raised his empty glass.

"Thank ye kindly," he said.

Gloria smiled. "You make friends easily, John. That's a good asset. Especially here."

"As I said, I try to be polite."

The bartender poured a drink for Jocko and then left, taking the bottle back with him to the other end of the bar.

"The night's still young, John, are you sure you want to go home so early?"

"I'm kind of tired."

"I can imagine. One of my men, Kurt Gruber, you haven't met him and he's not here tonight, tells me you brought three horses up with you when you came to town."

"That's right."

"Kurt said you left early this morning with those same horses and came back without them."

"This Kurt is very observant," Slocum said.

Gloria forced a smile.

"He keeps his eyes open. This is a small town. Not much can go on without somebody noticing."

"And probably a lot can go on without anyone at all noticing."

"What do you mean by that?"

"Nothing. All small towns are pretty much the same. People see what they want to see. Or, people don't see what they don't want to see. It's the same all over."

"I guess. You may be right. I was just wondering what you did with those three horses. Did you bring them up for a friend, perhaps?"

"They were just extra horses I had with me. On the ride up I met a rancher who offered to buy them from me. He was in the middle of roundup, and I told him I'd bring them down to him today."

"Oh, what rancher was this?" she asked.

"Charlie Naylor of the C Bar N," Slocum lied.

"Oh, good old Charlie. He comes in here now and again. He probably paid you a pretty good price."

"Yeah, he did," Slocum said, enjoying the lie now. At least Gloria had revealed that she was having him followed, or at the minimum watched, by Gruber. He wondered if Gruber had had anything to do with murdering Sally. Whoever those two men were that he had seen running from her house, they certainly had seen him riding up with those three horses. The only thing was that he had been going the wrong way. Surely, Gruber, if he'd seen him ride out of town that morning would have mentioned which direction he was going. He waited for Gloria to step into the big hole he had left for her.

"Funny," she said, "I didn't know Charlie had cows running up toward Yellowstone."

"I don't know where he made his gather."

"But you took the horses to him. I believe you said you ran them down to his ranch."

"I did," Slocum said.

"But Kurt saw you heading up the valley toward Yellowstone Park."

"I thought I'd see some country first."

"I see," she said, and Slocum knew that she didn't see at all. *Good*, he thought. Let her be suspicious of him. It would keep her off balance, maybe.

"Well, at least you're not hurting for money right now. You don't need an advance on your salary. A lot of men who come up here do."

"No, Gloria, I'm fine."

She tossed off her drink, which told Slocum she had other things on her mind and wanted to attend to them. She probably wanted to question Gruber again. Gruber would probably say he had been too busy running away after he and someone else, maybe Herb Duggins, had killed Sally Loving. The bastards.

Slocum tossed his drink down and stood up. He reached for his coat and slipped it on while Gloria watched him.

"I'll see you tomorrow afternoon," he said. "Thanks for the drink, Gloria."

"You're welcome. Good night."

As he turned to leave, Slocum felt through the pockets of the heavy winter coat.

"Oh, looky here," he said, fishing out the ducat that Gloria had given him the day before. "Here's that free drink chit you gave me."

He held it out to her.

Gloria stared at the ducat for several seconds. Then she quickly snatched it out of Slocum's hand.

"Never mind," she snapped. "You won't need it now."

"No, I reckon not," he said. He gathered up the ledger and abacus, then touched his index finger to the brim of his hat in a salute. As he walked toward the door, Jocko Cooley lifted a hand in farewell. Slocum nodded and continued across the floor. He felt Gloria's gaze on him the whole way. Outside, in the night, the cold chilled his face as a light breeze sprang up. His boots crunched on the frozen ground.

He looked back at the saloon, with its golden light spraying through the windows.

He smiled.

At least nobody was following him this time.

But he wondered where Kurt Gruber was on such a night. And he also wondered why Gloria had not mentioned Sally Loving and the way she had died. Surely, the whole town knew about her murder by now.

He had a hunch Gloria had known about it before anyone else besides himself, Gruber and Duggins.

It was just a hunch.

But Slocum relied on his hunches.

19

She stood in the doorway, waiting for him. Her lithe form was bathed in lamp-glow. The flimsy negligee she wore was transparent from the backlighting of the fire in the fireplace and the coal oil lamp.

"Grace?" Slocum said, as he walked toward the house. The sign outside creaked on its chains as a light breeze blew against its flat surface. The sound was eerie in the stillness. "You weren't waiting up for me, were you?"

"An old habit," she said, and her voice was soft as silk, thick with unspoken promise. "My husband Gordon used to go to the Silvertip to drink and play cards. I was worried about you."

"No need to worry," he said, as he stepped inside the door. She closed it behind them, then stepped up to him and put her arms around his neck. She kissed him.

"Ummm," she said. "I love the smell of whiskey on a man's breath."

Her kiss was warm and lusty. Slocum felt somewhat

flabbergasted. He hadn't expected such warmth and passion from a reserved lady like Grace Fletcher. But women were constantly surprising him that way.

"Let me help you out of that heavy coat, John."

Before he could reply, she was unbuttoning the bearskin coat and pushing it off of his shoulders. She took off his frock coat, too. Her hands touched the belly gun behind his belt buckle.

"My, that's hard," she said. "Is that a spare gun or have I aroused you so quickly."

Slocum swallowed a liquid lump in his throat. She let her hand slide down to his crotch and squeezed him there.

"Either you have two hideout pistols," she said, "or you are happy to see me."

"Yeah," he said. "I'm happy as hell, Grace. Just a little surprised, is all."

"A woman gets lonely, you know."

Before he knew fully what was happening, he was in her bedroom and she was taking off his shirt. She put his hideout pistol on a table and unbuckled his gunbelt. That coiled down to the floor and then she had his trousers halfway down his legs. She pushed him onto the bed, knelt down and removed his boots. Then she tugged his pants down the rest of the way and pulled on his shorts.

When she had him naked, there was no doubt that he was glad to see her. She slipped a couple of straps from her shoulders and her nightgown puddled on the floor at her bare feet.

Underneath the petticoats and aprons and full dresses, Grace was a most voluptuous woman. She stood there, letting Slocum drink in all the curves, the full breasts, the inviting patch between her legs. A single lamp illuminated her naked body. She smiled and put one leg next to the other in a provocative pose.

"Do you like what you see, John?"

"Yes. You're a very beautiful woman, Grace."

"Do you want me?" she asked in a coquettish tone of voice.

"Yes," he said, his voice husky, "I want you, Grace Fletcher. Come here and let me show you."

She melted into him on the bed, knocking him gently on his back. They embraced and kissed. The kiss was long and lingering. Then her hands began to explore him and each touch sent a current of pleasure through his own body. He touched her breasts and leaned forward, kissing each nipple, laving them with slow strokes of his tongue. Her body arched with pleasure and she pressed against him, rubbing her vagina up and down the length of his cock until it grew even more rigid.

They rolled over and faced each other, side to side, and her hand grasped his cock and squeezed it. He plied her cunt with his fingers and felt the rush of hot fluids as he entered her, stroking her clitoral button.

"Oh, yes, John," she breathed. "You make me so hot."

"You do the same to me," he said.

"I want you inside me, John. I'm ready."

She rolled away from him, out of his arms and flattened herself on the bed, spreading her legs wide to receive him. He arched over her and straddled her, then dipped his loins down, as she thrust her hips upward. She grasped his stalk and guided it to her portal. He pushed and slid inside her, his cock throbbing with engorged blood.

"Ah," she breathed, and then let out a little mewing sound as he delved deeper, sliding through moist silk. Her body convulsed with a sudden spasm as he reached the end of her tunnel, and she bucked with pleasure as he stroked back and forth, back and forth.

She clasped him in her arms and he felt the sting of her fingertips as they dug softly into his exposed back. Like cat's claws, those fingers of hers, slightly painful, but pleasurable as well. He drove into her with powerful thrusts and her fingernails raked his back, drawing blood, leaving furrows in his flesh.

She matched his thrusts with her own and their bodies made a smacking sound when they came together. Her bed creaked and groaned under the weight and strain of their lust.

"Faster," she said, and Slocum obliged her.

He was amazed at her stamina, at her eagerness to please him. She ground her hips against his and made them move in a circular motion as if to touch every inch of his prick with the yielding folds of her cunt. He drove into her with powerful strokes and she cried out and her fingernails dug into his buttocks as she pulled on him, pulled him down and against her with wiry strong arms.

"Oh, I'm coming, coming, John. Oh yes, I can feel it. Like electricity, like shock waves. So good, so damned good."

He exploded his balls inside her and she screamed with the heat and gush of it and he spewed his seed inside her while she writhed beneath him like a woman in torment, like a woman flailing in the sea and drowning.

Then she relaxed as he did, both of them spent, satiated,

their bodies slickened with sweat as if they had been oiled by some Roman slave in the days of Pompeii. She cooed with pleasure as he slumped against her, drained for the moment of all power.

"Thank you, John dear," she said. "Thank you so very very much. I feel like a woman again. Truly."

"You, Grace," he said, "were never anything but a woman. You give, my dear, as good as you get."

He rolled off her body and they lay there in a lassitude of their loving aftermath, both breathing deeply, she sighing as he uttered guttural grunts as a man will do after a stint of heavy labor. She reached over and put her hand on his flat stomach, let it lie there, weak as a wounded bird, while he put a hand on her leg and squeezed it reassuringly.

"Will you spend the night in my bed, John?" she asked. "I want you close to me. I want you again."

"Yes," he said, "but I have a favor to ask you before I forget it. And I may get up early. I have things to do tomorrow and I go to work at the Silvertip in the afternoon."

"Why, yes, of course," she said. "Any favor you ask. With pleasure."

"How well do you know the sheriff of this town?"

"Lonnie? Pretty well. Lonnie Pearsall. Why?"

"I want you to sound him out about the stage robberies prior to the Cheyenne company folding. I can't go there because I think someone will be watching me."

"What exactly do you want to know?" she asked.

"I need to know the exact dates of every robbery, going back to when they started. And I also want you to ask Pearsall if he has any suspects, how he feels about Gloria Vespa and her bunch, her establishment."

"I already know the answer to that," she said. "He suspects Gloria, and the men who work for her, of many crimes, including murder. But he's never been able to prove anything."

"Well, maybe I can get some proof for him."

"I know he'd be mighty grateful."

"Just get me that information, will you?"

"What are you going to do?"

"I'm going to start tracking," he said. "I'm going to follow a trail made out of paper."

"John, do you know much about Gloria Vespa? She's a dangerous woman."

"I know that much," he said.

"You know she's Italian. Her father was a gangster in New York or somewhere back East. He was killed, but he left her a lot of money. She came here a few years ago and took over the saloon business, drove most of the others here out of business."

"She's a tough lady."

"You must be careful. I think Gloria had my husband killed. I can't prove it, of course, but . . ."

He didn't follow up on it, but he figured Grace's husband had gotten involved with Gloria, either romantically or in business. It was time, he thought, that someone put Gloria out of business.

"I will," he said.

Before he dozed off to sleep, Grace asked him one last question.

"John, before you go to sleep, do you know what Gloria's name means?"

"Glory?"

"No, her last name."

"No. It's Italian, I gather."

"Yes. It means 'wasp.' "

"Wasp?"

"Yes, and she has a deadly sting."

20

Slocum went on the scout early the next morning. He saddled up Oro in the freezing cold and rode north toward the wild place that had been designated a national park in 1875, Yellowstone. He stayed well away from where he knew Hovis, Jenkins and the Crow were holed up. He rode off toward the mountain range and found the exact spot of the type he was looking for. Then he rode back into town and stopped at the undertaking parlor where he spoke to a man named Sol Levitz.

"I want to pay you for the funeral and burial of Sally Loving," Slocum said.

"Sheriff Pearsall said the lady had set aside money for her last wishes," the undertaker said. "H'ain't been paid yet, but . . ."

"That's all right, Mr. Levitz. I want to pay all costs for the final arrangements."

"Suit yourself, Mr. Slocum, H'ain't none of my business if'n you want to throw away your money."

"Does her brother have a plot in the cemetery?"

"Yes, and Miss Loving told me, in writing mind you, that she wanted to be buried next to him, rest his soul."

Slocum paid Levitz and left the undertaking parlor. That visit had been the most depressing place he had been since arriving in Jackson Hole. From there, he rode to the Grand Teton Freight Company's office, tied Oro to the hitch ring outside and walked up on the small boardwalk, then into the front office. The outside of the building was old, made of logs, with a false front of siding lumber, two-by-sixes, but the inside smelled of new pine, with a counter and desks, and tables and filing cabinets in back of that. And there was another door, which Slocum surmised led to a back office. It had the same kind of smoked glass pane as he had seen in the Silvertip the night before. A clerk at one of the desks looked up when Slocum walked in, set down his pencil and shuffled some papers before walking to the counter.

"Yes, sir, may I help you?" the young man asked. "I'm Hans Nordstrom. You have freight to haul?"

"Good morning," Slocum said, "Mr. Nordstrom. No, I don't have anything to ship . . ."

Slocum didn't finish his sentence because the back door to the other office opened and a large man came through it, heading for the counter in long strides, his boots landing heavily on the hardwood floor. The man had the body of a burly lumberjack, with wide shoulders and a bulky neck that was dwarfed by his large head. He wore no hat, and his hair was as wiry and full and tawny as a Texas tumbleweed. He was clean-shaven except for flared sideburns that mapped both cheeks. And he wore a gun on his hip.

"I will take care of this, Hans," the man said, with a trace of a Teutonic accent. German, perhaps, Slocum thought.

"Yes, sir, Mr. Gruber," the young man said, and melted back from the counter and took his seat at his desk.

"Now, what is it you want, Mr. Slocum?" Gruber said.

"I wanted to know when the next stage from Cheyenne would be in. Stage or freight wagon."

"Why do you want to know this?"

"I'm expecting a package."

"What is in the package?"

"I don't see that that is any of your business, Mr. Gruber. Is that your name, Gruber?"

"I am Kurt Gruber."

"Are you the owner of this company?" Slocum asked.

"I work here," Gruber said.

"Then maybe you can answer my question."

"If you will tell me what is being shipped to you, maybe I can tell you if it will be on the next stage, or on the freight wagon."

"Tools," Slocum said.

"Tools? What kind of tools?"

"Mining tools, shovels, pick-axes, spades, and the like."

"It is a big package, no?"

"Yes. Very big. Heavy."

"Are you a miner?"

"Not exactly. But I have a use for the tools."

"There is no mining up here."

"No matter. I need the tools."

"They sell such tools here in Jackson Hole. At the mercantile."

"I ordered these tools shipped before I came up here."

"Then you must have a use for such tools."

"I said I did."

"Slocum, I know who you are, or who you say you are. And I know you brought three horses up here. And I know you did not sell them to Charlie Naylor."

"It seems to me you know a lot about my business, Gruber."

"I do not think you are a bookkeeper, either, Slocum."

"Well, it seems we differ on a lot of things."

Gruber squared off, and for a moment Slocum thought he might bound over the counter and start laying those big ham fists of his into him. But Gruber controlled himself and just glared.

"As for the shipment, Slocum, there will only be one more stage up this way from Cheyenne before the snow flies, and I will notify you if your tools are on board. It depends on weight, the number of passengers and other freight."

"No more freight wagons?"

"I doubt it. The stage will be here at the end of the week, unless it snows again. Now, if you have no more business with us, I must get back to my own work."

"I'll be seeing you, Gruber. If my tools don't come, I'll buy what I need at the mercantile."

"Yes, Slocum. You will be seeing me. Count on it."

"I hope so," Slocum said, turning away from the counter. "I'd hate to have you come up behind me and shoot me in the back."

He slammed the door before Gruber could say anything

more. He climbed aboard Oro and rode down to the mercantile store that was in the middle of the next block.

Slocum felt some satisfaction over his visit to the freight company. He had accomplished at least two goals. He had established that the new outfit was owned or under the control of Gloria Vespa, because Kurt Gruber was obviously in charge of the operation. Secondly, he had aroused Gruber's suspicions that Slocum had come to Jackson Hole to either help find the gold hidden by the Crow, or to help them hide it. He was pretty sure that Gruber already knew that Sally Loving had given him a map that led him to where Hovis Benton and Wilbur Jenkins were holed up. He would soon make sure that Gruber and the others in Gloria's employ had such a map. Only it would be one that Slocum himself would draw.

Inside the mercantile store, Slocum bought two dozen sticks of dynamite, fuses, caps and a box of wooden matches. These, which he had the store owner put in a heavy box, he secured to the back of his saddle, lashing the box down with leather thongs in a diamond hitch so that it wouldn't fall off on the rough ride ahead.

Slocum made sure that he was not followed, and retraced his route up toward Yellowstone Park, then to the place he had selected. The place was ideal. It offered Slocum the cover he needed to carry out his final tasks, and it had the necessary features to draw Gruber and his henchman to an exact spot.

He worked quickly, after donning work gloves so that he could handle the dynamite. He had bought DuPont 60/40 dynamite sticks. These were coated with a substance that caused severe headaches if one handled the sticks barehanded and then rubbed it off on the forehead or face. Slocum took the large bowie knife from his boot and cut each dynamite stick in half, leaving the ends exposed to the mixture of sawdust and nitroglycerin. When he was finished, he took several of the half sticks and placed them strategically in the rocks above the place he had selected to lure his quarry within range of the explosion. He placed dynamite caps just inside the cut ends of the sticks. He made a semicircle of sticks over a large enough area so that the explosion would trigger not only a rockslide, but hurl stone projectiles in every direction.

When he was finished placing the sticks, he ran fuses to some of them, which he had placed four inches apart. He did this to make sure that the explosions were virtually simultaneous. He ran long fuses to a spot concealed in a growth of trees, well away from and behind the rock face of the mountain. He made sure that the yellow fuses could not be seen from below and then concealed the ends under a large flat stone. There, he also placed the box of wooden matches for later use.

Slocum rode back to town via a different route. He unsaddled his horse and left Oro at the livery, then walked to Mrs. Fletcher's Boarding House. She was gone when he arrived. He went to his room and took a blank piece of paper and placed it flat on his table. He began to draw a map like the one Hovis had drawn, only this time he did not use Lawrence, Kansas, as a template, but, instead, used the actual town of Jackson Hole and the surrounding landmarks. He chewed on jerky and hardtack as he drew the map, labeling each building and street, the trail leading directly to the spot where he had placed the dynamite.

A fool could follow his map, Slocum thought. All he had to do now was see to it that his drawing fell into the right hands. That would come at another time. For now, he had to make sure Sheriff Pearsall had the evidence he needed to charge Gloria Vespa with the crime of murder. Some of the evidence would depend on what Grace Fletcher found out from the sheriff. If Slocum's hunch was right, he would be able to tie Gloria to all the stage robberies as well as murder and the takeover of the stage route to Cheyenne.

When Slocum left to go to work at the Silvertip Saloon, he carried Jenkins' abacus with him and a sharpened pencil. He also carried the map he had drawn.

From now on, he knew, everything he accomplished depended on perfect timing. It was like a game of poker, with each bet carefully planned, each deal of the cards weighed and played. The only thing bothering him about all of it now was that Kurt Gruber was the wild card.

Gruber was more than suspicious. Slocum was sure that the man would be watching him like a hawk when he worked on the books at the saloon.

Let him watch, Slocum thought.

The hand was a hell of a lot quicker than the eye.

[illegible]

[illegible]

[illegible]

[illegible]

[illegible]

[illegible]

[illegible]

21

Gloria Vespa was at the saloon when Slocum arrived. She greeted him warmly enough, he thought, and led him to the back office where she showed him to a desk at which he presumed Wilbur had worked, before he escaped death by the skin of his teeth.

"I've tried to keep the books up," she said. "But I'm a little behind. There are two sets of books that you will work on." She showed him the ledgers. "One is for the Silvertip, the other is for another enterprise. You don't need to know the name of it. And you will also have two payrolls to do each week. It's a lot of work. Do you think you can handle it, John?"

"Yes, I'm sure I can, Gloria."

"You will not take any work home with you. What you do here, stays here."

"I understand."

"And all of this is confidential and private. I don't want outsiders to know my business."

"Nor will they," Slocum said. "Discretion is my middle name."

Gloria laughed. "I doubt that, but I'm sure you will be an asset to me."

Slocum sat at the desk. Gloria sat at another desk a few feet away. A short while later, Herb Duggins came in and bent down to whisper something to Gloria. The two spoke softly, their voices too low for Slocum to hear what they were saying, and then Gloria left. Herb took her place at the desk, glancing every so often over at Slocum, who was busy going through the ledgers, receipts and payroll. The bartender, Freddie Hewitt, came in every so often to speak to Herb, telling him it was, as usual, slow in the afternoon.

"It'll pick up when the sun goes down," Duggins said and resumed his work at the desk.

Slocum pored over the ledger containing bank deposits and payouts. It was the newest and had fewer entries than the ledger assigned to the Silvertip, but it was the one Slocum was most interested in examining. He made separate notes of the bank deposits and dates, sliding the page under others so that anyone stopping by would not see what he was doing. He still managed to make sense of the Silvertip ledger, and bring it up to date. He noted the salaries of all of Gloria's employees. Those salaries paid out of the income noted in the other ledger, the one without any identification, but which he suspected belonged to the freight operation, had only initials for payroll. But he was able to figure out who was being paid from those proceeds. At least some of them. He learned that he had not met everyone who worked for Gloria.

Some initials appeared for a while and then were dropped from the ledger. He could only guess what had happened to those employees.

Gruber came in late that afternoon with receipts, but by that time Slocum had concealed all of his notes in his boot. He had done that when Duggins left to take a leak. Gloria came in and said she was going to the hotel to oversee her staff in preparation for the evening meal.

"Maybe I'll see you tonight when I finish up and return to the Silvertip," she said.

"I don't know," Slocum said. "I may be bushed by then, Gloria."

"Well, you have a couple of free drinks coming, you know."

"I know. I'll try and stick around."

"Good. I'd like to go over the books and see how you've done before you go home for the night."

Slocum did stay after he finished work, but not because he wanted to take advantage of the two free drinks that went along with his salary. He was hoping to run into a man he had met the night before in order to enlist him in his elaborate scheme. He hated like hell to use an innocent man, but he had no choice. He knew he was running out of time. Gloria Vespa and her henchmen, Gruber and Duggins, were not stupid. They'd give him only so much rope and then they'd try to hang him.

Jocko Cooley was sitting at the bar when Slocum joined him after putting away his ledgers for the day.

"Buy you a drink, Jocko?" Slocum said, as he slid onto the stool next to Cooley's.

"Ah, for sure, friend John, you may. Especially if you're buyin' that good sippin' whiskey I tasted last night."

"You're a regular here, are you?"

"You've found me out."

Slocum laughed.

He motioned to Freddie Hewitt, who came over, seemingly without enthusiasm.

"Two drinks here, Freddie," Slocum said. "I'm buying Jocko's. Mine is free."

"I know, Slocum. Better enjoy Gloria's generosity while you can."

"What's that supposed to mean?"

"It means I don't think you'll be around here long, Slocum."

"You must know something I don't know, Freddie." Slocum's tone was amiable.

"I know I don't like you, and I think there's a long line right behind me."

"The drinks, Freddie. You can keep your comments to yourself."

Freddie grumbled, but brought out the bottle of Old Taylor and poured two drinks. He took the silver dollar Slocum flipped onto the bar and set spinning.

When Hewitt was out of earshot, Slocum leaned close to Cooley and whispered in his ear.

"Jocko, can you keep a secret?"

Cooley nodded.

"Would you like to make some money? Good money. Honest money."

"Sure," Cooley whispered.

"Do you know where Mrs. Fletcher's Boarding House is?"

"Sure do."

"Do you have a horse?"

"I do. An old nag I keep at my digs."

"Good. Meet me at Mrs. Fletcher's on Sunday morning. Early. About eight o'clock, saddled up and ready to ride."

"Where we goin'?" Cooley asked.

"To a place where we can dig up gold that's already been mined."

"Crow gold?" Cooley asked, much to Slocum's surprise.

"Yeah. I've got a map. I know where it's buried."

"I been hearin' about that," Cooley said. "Talk's died down of late, but . . ."

"Did you know Hovis Benton?"

"Yeah, I knowed him. When he worked here as a swamper, that's when I heard about hidden gold, hidden by a bunch of renegade Crow Injuns."

"Not a word about this, Jocko. But Hovis left me a map before he lit a shuck out of here."

"Is Hovis dead, then?"

Slocum didn't answer. He had planted the seed. He knew he couldn't safely make a move until Sunday when the whole Vespa bunch would be off and ready to take the bait. He was taking a chance on Cooley, but he felt he was a pretty good judge of men and the old prospector, he figured, was the right man for the job he had planned. Prospectors, he knew, thrived on gossip and rumors. And the mention of gold would start the wheels turning in Cooley's brain. His mouth, after a few drinks, would take care of the rest.

Slocum was counting on the word that he had a map to the hidden cache of gold doing the rest.

He finished his drink and patted Cooley on the back. He put a five-dollar bill on the bar top.

"Have yourself a night, Jocko. Don't forget about Sunday."

Slocum got up and Hewitt looked over at him.

"You got one drink coming, Slocum."

"You drink it, Freddie. I'm tired. Going home."

Slocum left before Gloria showed up, and walked quickly over the thawed ground to Grace's boardinghouse. There was still much to do, and he was anxious to learn what she had found out from Sheriff Pearsall that day.

The evening was clear and cold. Stars sprinkled the night sky, seeming very close in the high, thin air of the Grand Tetons. The Tetons were as majestic at night as they were imposing during the day.

"Have you eaten supper, John?" Grace asked when he came inside.

"Nope."

"I didn't expect you home this early. But I saved some food for you. It's still warm on the stove. I fixed mutton tonight."

Slocum's mouth watered.

"I could eat," he said.

"Very well, I'll set the table. I have lots and lots to tell you, and I hope it pleases you."

Slocum washed up and joined Grace in the kitchen, sitting at the table which was set for one. Grace served up the boiled mutton, with potatoes and string beans. She also served half a large peach in a small bowl.

"What did you find out from Sheriff Pearsall?" Slocum asked.

Grace sat across from him at the table.

"Much," she said. "But I've a surprise for you. Lonnie will be here around midnight. He thought it best to come that late so there was little likelihood of his being seen making a visit."

"So, he's made a connection between the downfall of the old freight company and the rise of the new?"

Grace pulled some papers out of the pocket of her apron and laid them on the table.

"These are the dates of the robberies when the old Cheyenne freight haulers were still coming up here to Jackson Hole."

Slocum looked at the figures on the paper and his eyebrows raised. His head was still full of the dates he had written down that day at the Silvertip.

He withdrew the papers from his boot and laid them alongside the ones Grace had brought him. He pushed his plate away and Grace cleared the table while he compared dates of the robberies with dates of bank deposits that he had taken from the ledger. She returned in a moment with two cups of coffee and set them down on the table.

"They match up," Slocum said. "It looks as if Gloria and her bunch had this well planned. They put the other freight company out of business while enriching her coffers, then took over the route so that they are now passing for a legitimate business."

"Lonnie will be pleased," she said. "He had a hunch that you were on the right track."

"What time is it?" Slocum asked.

Grace left the room and returned a moment later.

"It's midnight," she said. "Lonnie should be here very soon now."

Slocum sipped his coffee and pondered what he had discovered. Grace looked over the rim of her cup and smiled at him.

"I'm glad to see you happy, John. But you look very tired."

He was tired, but he was excited, too.

"Listen," she said. "I hear hoofbeats."

Slocum heard them, too, and then they stopped, right outside the house. A split second later, the silence was shattered by the crack of a rifle. They heard a loud thud and then a man shouted in a voice laden with agony.

"Help."

Slocum was already running for the door, drawing his Colt pistol in mid-stride.

Grace sat there at the kitchen table, frozen in fear.

22

The horse spooked when Slocum, in a crouch, ran up to the fallen man. It danced away backward, its reins trailing.

"Whoa, boy," Slocum growled as he knelt down.

"Shot, help me," the man said. He was lying on his side, holding one hand on his hip. Slocum looked around as he felt the wound. His left hand came away sticky with fresh hot blood.

"Sheriff?"

"Unh, yeah. Get me inside. I think he only nicked me."

"Do you know who shot you?" Slocum asked.

"No. Damned bushwhacker."

Slocum listened for any sound. It was quiet in the house and he knew Grace must be trembling with fear somewhere safe.

"I'm going to drag you past the hitchrail, Pearsall. See if we draw any fire. If not, I'll pack you inside. Can you hold on?"

"Bleedin' like a stuck pig, but I don't feel no bad pain."

Slocum kept his cocked Colt at the ready as he dragged the sheriff toward the house with one hand. He waited a few seconds, looking all around for any movement, then let the hammer down on his pistol and rammed it into its holster. He put his arms under the wounded man's legs and back, and lifted him with a clean jerk, then waddled, low, inside the house. He kicked the door shut with his boot and carried Pearsall over to the divan, but laid him on the floor, flat on his back.

"You just hold tight, Pearsall," Slocum said, "while I check this wound. Grace," he called, "bring some towels and alcohol."

Slocum heard movement in the kitchen as he bent over and turned the sheriff slightly onto his good side. In the light from the lamp, he saw a bloody furrow in the sheriff's side. It wasn't bleeding much now, only seeping, but the wound looked as if someone had gouged out a path with a blunt instrument through the roll of fat just to the side of the abdomen.

"You're not bleeding much now, Pearsall. I think I can dress this wound and have you back on your feet in no time. I'll get you a swallow of whiskey while we go through this."

"Thanks. You Slocum?"

Slocum nodded.

Grace rushed in to the front room with towels and a bottle of rubbing alcohol.

"Do you need some hot water?" she asked, turning her head so that she could not see the sheriff's wound. "I've got a pot set on the stove to boil. Won't be a minute."

"That might help. Go in my room and look in my saddlebags or on the dresser. There's a bottle of whiskey in there you can bring."

"Be right back," she said.

Slocum touched one of the towels to the open wound, pressing down gently. The sheriff winced and stifled a cry of pain.

Grace returned with the bottle of whiskey she had found in Slocum's room. "The hot water should be ready," she said. "I'll fetch it."

Slocum uncorked the bottle and let some whiskey seep through Pearsall's lips. The sheriff's complexion was pale from the shock of the bullet that had plowed a furrow through his flesh. The whiskey brought some of the color back to his cheeks. Pearsall groaned in gratitude as Slocum soaked up all the seeping blood with fresh towels. He poured rubbing alcohol into the gouge and the sheriff nearly jumped up off the floor. But Pearsall bit down and got in control of himself.

Finally, Slocum bathed the wound in hot water, then, with bandages Grace brought him, he bound up the wound, wrapping gauze around Pearsall's torso.

"There, Pearsall," Slocum said. "I put some unguent on that bandage that should help with the healing. Feel like sitting up? Maybe on the divan there, where you'll feel a mite more comfortable?"

"Help me up," Pearsall said, holding up an arm.

Slocum pulled the sheriff to his feet and helped him to the divan.

"Well, that's quite a turn," Pearsall said. "I came a roundabout way, but somebody must have followed me. First time I've ever been dry-gulched."

"You were lucky," Slocum said.

Grace sat down, a look of concern on her face. Slocum squatted on the floor, then stood up.

"Who do you think shot you, Sheriff?" Slocum asked.

Pearsall shrugged. "Gruber or Duggins, maybe. They're the town toughs and they are high on my list of suspects in my investigation of a string of murders. That would be my guess. One or t'other."

"Grace," Slocum said, "would you bring those papers in from the kitchen, please? I'd like the sheriff to take a look at them."

"Of course," she said.

Grace returned in a few moments with the papers. Slocum took them from her and showed them to Pearsall. He examined them carefully as Slocum pointed out the dates and the sets of figures he had recorded. The sheriff finished and looked at Slocum.

"It seems pretty clear," Pearsall said. "This was all planned. The robberies, the murders. And it all leads back to Gloria Vespa."

"You keep those, Pearsall," Slocum said. "By Monday, this may all be over and you may have your town back again."

"What are you getting at, Slocum?"

"I can't tell you right now. Just take it easy and rest up. Tomorrow's Saturday and I think it will be my last day at work for Gloria Vespa."

"What about Sunday?" Grace said. "You'll be here?"

"I'm leaving early Sunday morning. I may have some news for both of you by nightfall."

Grace and Pearsall looked at Slocum with puzzled expressions on their faces.

But Slocum didn't say a word. He was already thinking about what he was going to do the next day. Everything depended on him making just the right moves.

And a lot depended on Gloria Vespa and her greedy black heart.

23

Slocum rode Oro into town on Saturday morning. He stopped at the mercantile and bought a pick and a shovel, and tied them crossways on the back of his saddle, atop his bedroll, in plain view. He had the map he had made in an outside pocket of his frock coat, where part of it was visible as a folded sheet of paper with black markings showing through. Anyone looking closely at it could see that it was a map. Inside the fold, Slocum had put two very small pieces of thread which he had gotten from Grace's sewing kit. Both were black and difficult to see.

He got to the Silvertip just before noon and left his horse tied to one of the hitchrails. Then he went inside and got to work on the books. He took off his frock coat and hung it on a wooden peg outside the office.

Freddie Hewitt arrived shortly after noon and worked behind the bar, dusting, setting out bottles, making sure all the glass and the bar top sparkled. Herb Duggins came in around one o'clock, looking as if he was hungover.

"You missed a lot last night, Slocum," Duggins said. "The place was packed. It gets that way just before winter when people think they're going to get snowed in without any liquor or good times."

"So, business drops off after the snow flies?"

"Nope. Hell, people come in here with snowshoes on, sleighs, you name it. And they come in early when the fire's a-roarin' and the whiskey's flowin'. Don't sell as much beer, but the whiskey more'n makes up for it. And the cards. People just love to play cards on cold winter days."

"I guess it evens out," Slocum said.

"Say, is that your horse outside, the sorrel gelding?"

"Yeah."

"You plannin' on doin' some tillin'? I noticed you got a pick and shovel. They look brand new."

"I was expecting a box of tools from Cheyenne. Can't wait any longer."

Slocum worked through all the comings and goings of Gloria, Kurt Gruber and Freddie, and kept his nose in the books.

"Your box of tools didn't come in this mornin'," Gruber said to Slocum. "That's the last stage from Cheyenne. Snow'll be flyin' in a few days, from the look of the clouds buildin' up over the Tetons."

"Yeah, well, I can't wait any longer," Slocum said.

"Um, that why you bought yourself a pick-axe and a shovel?"

"That's my business," Slocum said.

"You'll dig in hard ground up here, Slocum," Gruber said.

"Maybe not so hard, Gruber."

Gruber shot Slocum a look and then grumped out of the office.

Slocum heard a lot of whispering that afternoon, especially when Duggins got called out by Freddie. He heard Gloria's voice, too. A lot of rustlings and then some awkward conversations with both Freddie and Duggins, later on. Gloria was drippingly sweet to him, but he knew her talk was like a pasted-on smile, without any warmth or meaning.

"You can go home early, today, John," she said, as she was leaving to return to the hotel. "You should be almost caught up by now."

"Thanks, Gloria," he said. "My eyes are plumb wore down to nubs. And I've got a busy day tomorrow."

"Oh? Doing what?"

"Going for a ride," he said. "Early."

"Well, don't work too hard. Go home and get some rest."

It was nearly dark by then, and Slocum was hungry. He hadn't eaten since breakfast.

Slocum left shortly after Gloria did and was surprised to run into Gruber at the bar. He was drinking a beer and had a look of smug satisfaction on his face.

"You forgot your coat, Slocum," Freddie said, a funny look on his face.

"Oh, yeah. Thanks, Freddie."

Slocum walked back and took his frock coat off the peg. He slipped it on and tapped the map loudly as if to make sure it was still there. Then he walked toward the door. Gruber put out an arm and stopped him as he passed by.

"Slocum, Gloria said you used that pistol you wear for hammerin' nails. Ain't no carpentry work around here."

Looking him straight in the eyes, Slocum said, "I use it to kill snakes, too, Gruber."

He walked out and climbed on his horse. He rode straight to Mrs. Fletcher's and, once inside his room, he took out the map and looked at it. He smiled.

Both pieces of thread were gone. And neither was in his pocket, which he turned inside out and shook over the clean tabletop.

"I wonder who they got to copy my map?" Slocum said aloud. "I just hope you did it right, whoever you are."

He hoped Gloria and the Silvertip would have a busy Saturday night, because they would have their work cut out for them tomorrow when they followed the directions on the map.

Slocum knew he would be busy, too.

Killing was such a lot of work, especially on his day off.

24

Slocum waited for Jocko Cooley, mulling over what he must do. He recalled what Old Eagle had told him when the Crow brave was leading him back to Jackson Hole.

"You want me come, Slocum, you make smoke. You make blanket smoke. You savvy blanket smoke?"

"Yes."

"You make smoke, we come. We fight good."

"And you will bring Hovis and Wilbur with you?"

"They come, too. Heap plenty brave come. You make smoke."

He was counting on it. He might not need the Crow, but they wouldn't be in the way.

Grace was awake, but he told her he didn't want to eat breakfast.

"I'm going hunting," he said. "I hunt better on an empty stomach."

"I dread to ask what you will be hunting. Sheriff Pearsall begged to come with you."

"He can help best by staying in town, for now," Slocum said. "But you can do me a big favor, if you would."

"Gladly," she said.

"Tell Pearsall to get a wagon ready and round up as many deputies as he can. Tell him to wait and keep his eyes on the north rim of the Tetons. When he hears a big explosion, tell him to bring the wagon and his deputies as fast as he can to that place."

Grace shuddered and Slocum felt a pang of guilt. He would have liked to have confided in her more fully, but what she didn't know couldn't hurt her. And he cared for her. Very much. She was a sweet, lonely woman, and deserved better. She had been hurt by Gloria Vespa and her gang as much as anyone in Jackson Hole.

Jocko arrived at first light, mounted on a sorry, swaybacked horse that had to be at least ten years old, but was probably closer to twelve or fifteen. But he had a rifle with him and an old converted Remington .44 New Model army pistol tucked in his belt. He wore a cartridge belt, too.

"You've got a Henry," Slocum said. "Haven't seen one of those in quite a spell.

"It's a 44/70 Yellow Boy and it shoots straight as a honeybee flies."

"Let's head out," Slocum said. He was saddled and ready to go. He waved good-bye to Grace, who stood on the porch, and saw her turn away as her eyes flooded with tears.

"Where we goin', Slocum?" Cooley asked.

"Into the jaws of death, Jocko."

"Sonofabitch. I should have got drunk last night."

"You can get drunk tonight. I'm buying," Slocum said.

They came to the place where Slocum had set his trap. In the distance, they could hear the church bells ring in Jackson Hole, and in the east, the sky was a crimson holocaust, a sailors' warning dawn breaking over the jagged peaks of the towering Tetons. The sky to the west was scudding up with clouds. Unless Slocum missed his guess, there would be fresh snow on the high peaks by the next day and maybe down on the flat, as well.

"Need me for anything?" Jocko asked when Slocum dismounted and started untying the thongs that held the pick and shovel to his saddle.

"No, just sit tight, Jocko. You'll get your turn. I want to set these out first, then we ride to higher ground."

Slocum stuck the shovel into the ground so that it stood upright and was easily visible. Then he buried the spiked end of the pick-axe in another spot, and left it canted so that it also could be seen by anyone riding up close. He mounted Oro and set out for the place where he had run the fuses and left the box of matches. Jocko followed him.

Up on the rimrock, behind the trees, Slocum dismounted and told Jocko to tie up his horse and join him.

"You're settin' some kind of trap, ain't ye, Slocum?"

"Yes."

Slocum moved the rock where he had put the ends of the fuses. Jocko leaned over, saw them, and whistled low in his throat.

"What you got out there, dynamite?"

Slocum nodded and tied two fuses together, with the ends close together. A single match should be able to light both.

"What the hell are you trying to do?" Jocko asked.

"I made a map to this place and someone at the Silver-tip filched it from my pocket and copied it. They'll think gold is buried down there and will, I hope, come to try and steal it."

"This ain't fair, Slocum. You're actin' as judge, jury and executioner, 'thouten no trial."

"I don't figure this blast will kill them," Slocum said. "Just cripple them enough so that they can stand trial."

"For what? Gamblin'?"

"No, for murder. For a lot of murders."

When he was finished, Slocum led Jocko and their horses up the mountain and off to a flat place. There, he tied Oro behind some spruce trees and told Jocko to do the same with his horse.

"Now, we gather firewood," Slocum said.

"Firewood?"

"The driest you can find."

Slocum built the fire and when it started to smoke, he got his bedroll off his horse, and brought it and the Greener back to the fire. He folded his blanket and laid it atop the smoking wood. He flipped it on and off, sending white puffs of smoke high in the air.

Jocko scratched his head.

"What in hell are you doin' Slocum? Tryin' to start an Injun war?"

"Sending for help, I hope."

When he was finished, Slocum put his bedroll back on his horse and kept the Greener. He and Jocko walked back to the place where he had set the fuses.

"Now what?" Jocko asked.

"Now, we wait. And watch."

They waited an hour. Slocum smoked and Jocko accepted a cheroot and joined him. They waited, into the next hour.

"Maybe they ain't a-comin'," Jocko said.

Slocum's gaze was toward town, fixed on the trail he had mapped out for his quarry. Movement caught his eye.

"No," he said to Jocko, "they're coming. The whole damned bunch of them."

The two men flattened out and peered downward from their hiding place. Slocum took out a match and laid it atop the matchbox with the box's sandpaper side up. His hands started to sweat and he dried them on his trousers. He put out his cheroot and nodded to Jocko to do the same.

They were all there, every mother's son of them, and the queen herself, the Teton temptress, Gloria Vespa. In the lead was Gruber, followed by his man at the freight office, Hans Nordstrom, then Freddie Hewitt and Gloria, riding side by side, trailed by Herb Duggins. And all were armed to the teeth.

He heard Gruber shout out something and then point to the place where the shovel and pick stood up, their handles stark against the rock face of the mountain.

"Spread out," Gruber called and the outlaws approached the spot with rifles and pistols at the ready. They formed a line, but were all riding close.

"They're comin'," Jocko whispered. "What you got that fuse set fer?"

"It's a quick fuse. Once they get in position I'll light it."

The armed force halted about fifty yards away from where Slocum had planted the tools. Gruber conferred with Gloria and Duggins. For a moment, Slocum thought they might turn back and avoid his trap.

"Slocum?" It was Gruber, calling out his name.

His voice bounced off the rock and died.

"Let's go up there," Duggins said. "Maybe he ain't found it yet."

"I don't like it none," Gruber growled.

More talk. More discussion. Then Gruber issued his orders.

The whole bunch rode up and dismounted. They all walked over to the shovel and looked down at the ground. Freddie pulled on the pick and snatched it out of the ground.

Slocum struck the match and lit the fuse. He could hear its soft hiss as the sputtering flame raced along the side of the mountain.

"Come on, Jocko," Slocum said. "Let's get behind a big rock."

He and Jocko scooted backward and took shelter. Slocum could no longer hear the fuse burning.

Suddenly, the mountainside exploded. It made one big roar and rocks came hurtling out in all directions, and rained down on the group assembled below. Slocum heard Gloria scream, and he heard men yell in pain. Rocks whistled over his and Jocko's heads, and smashed through spruce and pine and juniper like rocketing cannonballs.

The roar was tremendous and a great cloud of dust and smoke rose in the air.

Then, silence.

Slocum heard a noise behind him and turned around to see the face of Old Eagle. The Crow was grinning.

"Me track from smoke," he said.

A moment later, other Crow appeared, and behind

them, Hovis, grinning from ear to ear, strode up with Jenkins in tow.

"Let's get down there," Slocum said. "It's roundup time."

Slocum had them all laid out by the time the sheriff arrived with four deputies and a covered wagon. Freddie Hewitt was in bad shape, close to death. The others were badly hurt, but all alive.

"Sheriff, have you got enough evidence to charge these people with all those murders?" Slocum asked.

"You bet. I've got enough to hang them all. My God, what happened here, a war?"

Slocum smiled.

"Remember what General Sherman said, Pearsall? War is hell. And this is hell."

Later, Hovis told Slocum that they had moved the Crow gold to a safe place and would divide up their shares whenever he was ready.

"Send it to me," Slocum said. "I'm riding down the mountain tonight before I get snowed in."

"You could spend the winter in worse places, John."

"I know. But I've got cabin fever already." He looked up at the Tetons rising above them in granite majesty. "I feel caged in up here."

Saying good-bye to Grace was hard, but it was nothing new to Slocum. It was always hard to leave. But he knew his destiny better than most men.

Slocum rode alone.

Watch for

SLOCUM AND THE SLANDERER

311th novel in the exciting SLOCUM series from Jove

Coming in January!